Dark Side of the New Year

Riddhi Joshi

Hope you enjoy this book!!

Riddhi Joshi.

FanatiXx Publication

FanatiXx® Publication

AM/56, Basanti Colony, Rourkela 769012, Odisha

ISO 9001:2015 Certified

© Copyright, 2023 Riddhi Joshi

All rights reserved. No part of this book may be reproduced, stored in a retrieval system, or transmitted, in any form by any means, electronic, mechanical, magnetic, optical, chemical, manual, photocopying, recording, or otherwise, without the prior written consent of the author.

By: Riddhi Joshi

ISBN: 978-93-5605-255-0

Book: Dark Side of the New Year

Price: INR 199/-

Cover By: Noorleen Kaur Bhatia

Book Formatting by Hemant Bansal

Printing By: BooksClub.in

The opinions/ contents expressed in this book are the sole of the author and do not represent the opinions/ stands/ thoughts of FanatiXx® or any of its associates and affiliations.

DISCLAIMER

All rights reserved. This book may not be reproduced in whole or in part, or transmitted in any form, without written permission from the publisher, nor may any part of this book be reproduced, stored in a retrieval system, or transmitted in any form or by any means electronic, mechanical, photocopying, microfilming, and recording without written permission from the publisher.

Author assures that all content is original and he/she has full rights to publish and distribute the same. In any case of plagiarism, the publisher is not liable.

ACKNOWLEDGEMENT

If you are reading this page, then thank you for reading this book.

I would like to take a moment to thank my family and friends who inspired me to achieve more in my life. This book is a gesture of gratitude to my family and friends. 'You lose friends as you grow,' and here I have those few friends who stood by me for this book.

This wouldn't have been possible without the support of the publishing house. I would like to thank the entire publishing team that worked on the backend of my book.

CONTENT

DISCLAIMER _____ iii

ACKNOWLEDGEMENT _____ iv

Chapter 1 New Year New Beginning _____ 1

Chapter 2 Unexpected Events _____ 7

Chapter 3 Nightmares _____ 25

Chapter 4 Fabricated Stories _____ 41

Chapter 5 A Secret Revelation _____ 51

Chapter 6 The Long-Lost Truth _____ 63

Chapter 7 An Attempt To Murder _____ 87

Chapter 8 Paying For Your Sins _____ 99

Chapter 1
New Year
New Beginning

On New Year's Eve, an atmosphere of joyful anticipation permeated Sarah's household. The countenances of those present bore an expression of utmost cheerfulness. Sarah was meticulously preparing a delectable lasagna for her beloved parents. As the clock neared 8 p.m., the family convened around the dinner table, and Sarah's parents gazed upon her with astonishment and pride. "I am still unable to believe how fast our daughter has matured, blossoming into such an exceptional chef", her father expressed in a state of disbelief. Sarah, rejoiced by her father's heartfelt appreciation, responded with a light-hearted laugh, "Oh, Dad, please stop being so melodramatic."

Following the conclusion of the meal, all members of the family collaborated to clear the dining table. Sarah informs her parents, "I have made arrangements to celebrate the arrival of the New Year with my friends, so I will be leaving around 10 p.m." Her parents replied, certainly dear, make the best memories out there!

Watching her reflection in the mirror, adorned in an elegant black sequin dress, she exuded an aura of radiant bliss simultaneously she is engaged in applying her makeup. Sarah complemented her attire with a splendid new pair of high-heeled shoes, which she bought from her favourite brand. These black shoes enhanced her physical stature, standing at an impressive height of 5'6" and possessing a well-maintained physique with a weight of approximately 54 kilograms.

She received a praise from her mother, "You look so stunning, my dear as if you could effortlessly claim the title of Miss Universe!"

Sarah hugs her mother with smiling face and says "Thank you mom, you are the prettiest of all! I will be home around

4 a.m. so don't wait and sleep peacefully" saying so she leaves her home for the party.

As the clock struck 10 p.m., Sarah bid left home to enjoy the enchanting city of Paris, known as the City of Love, which seemed to transform into a radiant beacon of lights tonight. The jubilant atmosphere was palpable as the sounds of revelry filled her ears—It's the New Year, 2022! She boards a cab to reach the club, where the driver is eager to have a polite conversation,

"Madam, may I inquire about the field in which you have completed your education"?

Sarah responded, "I have attained a Master's degree in Fashion Designing from a prestigious university, where I was honoured with numerous awards and scholarships. Although, it was not required as I belong to a wealthy family. Currently, I am employed as an assistant buyer at my favourite brand, enjoying a lucrative salary."

Curious to learn more about the driver's life, Sarah questioned,

"May I ask your name?"

To which he humbly replied, "My name is Michael."

Dark Side of the New Year

Observing his anxious habit of nail-biting during their conversation, she gently inquired, "Could you share more about your life, sir?", with a mixture of vulnerability and resilience, began recounting his life's tumultuous journey.

"Once, I was a prosperous business tycoon. However, instead of bestowing blessings upon me, life subjected me to relentless hardships. Tragedy struck when my wife met a fatal accident, and my daughter was tragically dragged away from my life. She was too young to retain memories of me. A fabricated case was perpetrated against me resulted in the courts, as well as my extended family decided that it was in the best interest of the young girl not to dwell her in my darkness. Consequently, custody rights were granted to my younger cousin. My existence became a sleepless void as my business empire crumbled before my eyes. Struggling to regain control, I found myself unjustly incarcerated and rendered voiceless for an entire year. Witnessing my life spiral into disarray left me utterly helpless."

Sarah's radiant smile transformed into an expression of sadness upon hearing Michael's heartbreaking past. Attempting to console her, he reassured,

"Do not dwell in sorrow, madam. It has been nearly two decades since I lost everything, and I have found solace in my circumstances. I now drive a taxi as a means of diversion and livelihood."

Suddenly, a voice emanated from the navigation system, "Your destination has arrived."

Overwhelmed with empathy, she said goodbye Michael! Extending her best wishes for his future endeavours, and generously tipped him.

He gratefully expressed adding, "Please do not hesitate to reach out if I can be of any help." Sarah, with a composed voice replied, "Sure, thank you."

Dark Side of the New Year

Chapter 2
Unexpected Events

In a sudden shift of events, the weather transforms from a musical night of new year to a snowy night, with thunderstorms. Sensing the urgency, Sarah hastily made her way towards the club. As she waited for her friends within the club's confines, she decided to order a mocktail for herself at 10:30 pm. An hour passed by, yet her friends failed to show up, which was fuelling her anger and frustration; she took her mobile phone from her handbag, and discovered a staggering count of 15 missed calls from her friends. In a state of ire, she dialled Andrew's number and interrogated,

Dark Side of the New Year

"What is the matter, Andrew? Where have you all disappeared to? I have been waiting here for an hour!"

Andrew, with a sense of urgency in his voice, proceeded to explain the predicament, stating, "We all departed together in the same cab, but Nancy received a call from her father, informing her that her mother was admitted to the hospital. Consequently, we promptly rushed to the hospital."

Sarah, overcome with panic, and said, "I will be there shortly, please send me the address" Swiftly leaving the club, she hailed a taxi and made her way to the hospital.

Upon arriving at the hospital, Sarah approached the administration desk, beseeching the staff member, "Could you kindly provide information regarding the patient named Mehak, who was recently admitted?" The person in charge relayed the distressing news that, Mrs. Bernard, is currently in the ICU due to her critical condition. She meets her friends, and consoles Nancy about the situation; and sought further details regarding the incident. Nancy's father, feeling distraught, explained that his wife had a history of high blood pressure. While enjoying the weather from the terrace, she tragically slipped and fell. The doctors had conducted various tests, and the results are still pending. Together, they gathered in unity, fervently hoping that the dawn of the new year would not deliver disheartening news to their beloved family.

The room fell into a state of profound shock and sorrow when the doctor finally emerged with the test results. Nancy let out a heart-wrenching cry and hugged her father. While Sarah overcome by the weight of the situation, lost consciousness and slipped into a dreamlike state. In this dream, Michael appeared, attempting to draw her near, his touch tugging at her waist. Andrew swiftly revived her by gently sprinkling water on her face. As Sarah regained consciousness, she anxiously inquired about the test results. Andrew, replied that Nancy's mother had been diagnosed with paralysis, and the doctors offered no specific timeline for her recovery. Sarah hugged Nancy, offering words of comfort in an attempt to assuage her pain.

The group proceeded to the ICU in support of Nancy and her family; their eyes were brimming with tears. They spent the entire night together in that room, holding a silent vigil for Nancy's ailing mother. The following morning, around 7 a.m., the doctor requested that Mr. Bernard complete the discharge formalities for Mrs. Bernard. Accompanied by the doctor, he made his way to the administrative office, where he completed the necessary paperwork and settled the bills. Afterwards, he visited the medical store to procure the prescribed medications for his wife.

Dark Side of the New Year

Sarah was seated on the floor in a secluded corner of the ICU, gazing at the wall in silence. Lost and deprived of sleep throughout the night, she exhibited a profound sense of despair. Andrew, who sat beside her, reached out and held her hand in an attempt to ascertain the cause of her distress. With genuine concern, he addressed her,

"Sarah, it is understandable to feel disheartened by the circumstance we are currently in. However, we must forge ahead in life, don't you think? Consider Nancy's situation. We must provide support and assist our friend through this phase by motivating her. So, please gather yourself; and let's be there for Nancy." Andrew then embraced Sarah.

Sarah confided in Andrew about her conversation with Michael in the cab and the dream she experienced before fainting. Andrew, observing Sarah intently, reassured her, saying,

"Do not fret over it. Dreams do not reflect reality. Forget everything you saw and focus on advancing your career. Moreover, you must be there for Nancy during this challenging time."

Sarah began to feel a sense of relief and expressed her gratitude to Andrew, stating, "Thank you, Andrew. I feel much better now."

She proceeded to approach Nancy, who was unable to utter a word and hugged her, offering her companionship until her father arrived. Nancy's father informed them, "I have completed all the necessary procedures, and we can now take Mehak with us. Nancy, you must remain strong. Speak to your mother with a cheerful tone so that she may recover soon."

The entire group exited the hospital, with Mehak comfortably seated in a wheelchair, and arrived at Nancy's residence. Sarah noticed Michael was busy in car cleaning, but she chose to disregard his presence, entering the elevator with everyone else, while Michael remained oblivious to Sarah's presence. Upon entering the apartment where Nancy and her family lived, Sarah received a phone call from her mother. Concerned for her daughter, Mrs. Garcia inquired,

"Where are you, dear? You're not home yet, and it's already 9 a.m. instead of 4."

Sarah proceeded to explain the situation about Nancy's mother and reassured her mother, saying, "I will be home by evening."

Mrs. Garcia asked Sarah, "Dear, can you please return home as soon as possible, I'm feeling fatigued." Sarah's phone was

Dark Side of the New Year

on speaker mode, when Mr. Bernard interjected taking the phone from her, and assured Mrs. Garcia to not worry about Sarah. He says, "I will ask Andrew to accompany her and ensure she reaches home safely." Although Mrs. Garcia concealed her concerns during the call, she expressed gratitude to Mr. Bernard, hoping for Mehak's speedy recovery. Mr. Bernard reciprocated the gratitude and urged Mrs. Garcia to take care of herself. Andrew and Sarah met Nancy, advising her to take care of herself and emphasizing her importance of being present for her mother. Sarah promised to visit Nancy every day, to which Nancy nodded in agreement, and they left her residence.

Andrew and Sarah proceeded towards Andrew's car when suddenly Michael caught sight of Sarah, causing her to pause. He approached her and said, "Hey!". Sarah greeted Michael with a simple "Hi." Noticing Sarah's troubled expression, Michael inquired, "Is everything alright, Sarah?" In response, Sarah shared her concerns regarding Nancy's family and her mother. Michael expressed his worry for both mothers and proceeded to console Sarah by recounting how his wife used to comfort her younger sister. He explained that his wife would take her sister to various religious places, encouraging her to express gratitude for everything they had. Additionally, they would visit downtown areas to donate food to the homeless, which always brought a smile to her sister's face and lifted her spirits. Michael suggested Sarah to try the same approach.

Andrew arrived in his car and called out to Sarah. She assured Michael that she would give his method a try, and got into the car with Andrew. Curious about Sarah's whereabouts, Andrew asked, "Where were you?" Sarah explained that she was near the staircase having a conversation with Michael, whom she had mentioned earlier in the hospital. She also mentioned the method he had suggested for overcoming the trauma. Andrew commented, "Michael seems like a genuine person. You should try what he mentioned." Sarah agreed, saying, "Yeah, it sounds good. I will definitely give it a try!".

They proceeded towards the nearest temple and then visited a church. At each location, Sarah offered prayers, seeking courage for herself and Nancy to overcome the obstacles they faced. Then They headed towards a shopping street, where they bought a bag full of food packets. Continuing their journey, they arrived at the downtown area where many homeless people could be found. Sarah distributed the food packets to the children, witnessing their immediate joy and felt a sense of fulfilment. Andrew and Sarah left the location and arrived at Sarah's home.

Sarah invited Andrew to come upstairs as they rang the doorbell, Mrs. Garcia peeked through the keyhole; her initial smile turned into a tense expression. However, she opened the door with a smile and warmly welcomed both of them. Sarah introduced Andrew to her mother, and Mrs. Garcia

Dark Side of the New Year

invited him to have a seat. She asked Andrew if he would like some coffee, but Sarah interrupted. In a worrisome tone she asked her mother what had happened and why she urgently called her home? Mrs. Garcia explained, "My blood pressure became unstable, making me feel restless, and I was about to faint; that is why I called you." Sarah asked her mother to sit with Andrew while she prepared coffee. Eventually, the three of them sat together, sipping their coffee and discussing Mrs. Bernard's condition, offering prayers for her swift recovery. Andrew waved at Sarah and her mother before leaving the house. Mrs. Garcia appeared relieved as she watched Andrew depart while privately considering that it might have been for the best that he left soon. Meanwhile, Sarah busied herself with preparing lunch ahead of her 1 p.m. meeting at the office.

Upon arriving, to her surprise, she found Andrew was already there. Perplexed she asked him, "What are you doing in my office?" Andrew revealed that he has joined the same company and has been appointed her manager. Sarah's face lit up with happiness for him. She exclaimed, "Oh, that's great Andrew, Congratulations on your new job role!" He graciously thanked her and mentioned about a party that he had organized to celebrate his new job, scheduled for 7 p.m. Andrew looked quite charming with a well-built physique from his background as a gymnast, stood tall at 6'1" and possessed light brown eyes. Sarah responded,

"I will try to come, but I can't make any promises as I already have plans with my mom."

Andrew attempted to convince her by saying, "Can't you please join the party and postpone your plans? Come on; we are good friends."

However, Sarah expressed her regrets, stating, "I'm sorry, Andrew, but I won't be able to change the plans unless my mom changes her plan. I had already postponed them from yesterday." Disappointed, Andrew replied, "Sure, no problem."

They resumed their work. Later, Sarah led a meeting focused on attracting new investors for the company. She excelled in her presentation, receiving praise from the entire team. The investors were satisfied with the project and said they would respond within 24 hours regarding a potential investment. Sarah received a phone call from her mother, who apologised and explained that an old friend had unexpectedly come over, leading them to postpone shopping. Sarah replied, "No problem, Mom. If you have plans today, I will likely attend the party organised by Andrew to celebrate his new job in our company." Her mother appeared nervous and worried, but she responded, Sure, dear, but please make sure to return home by 11 p.m." Sarah replied, "Fine, Mom. Don't worry." Andrew approached Sarah and congratulated her on the impressive manner in which she had conducted the meeting. She graciously thanked him and informed him that her mother had cancelled their plan. And she would be able to attend the party in the evening. Andrew replied, "I'll be waiting for you, sweetheart!"

Andrew patiently waited for Sarah in the parking lot, holding a bouquet of flowers, Orchids. As Sarah approached the elevator, the doors opened on the ground floor where Andrew stood. He extended the bouquet towards her, and upon receiving it, Sarah exclaimed, "Oh my God! My favourite flowers! Thank you, Andrew, for such a thoughtful gesture." Andrew replied, "My pleasure, ma'am. Let's go." They both entered the car and embarked on their way to the party.

During the journey, Andrew continued showering Sarah with compliments, praising her meeting performance and her beauty. Sarah enjoyed the conversation and expressed her gratitude while she smiled at Andrew to tone down the cheesiness. Andrew eventually stopped the car near the Eiffel Tower, and as he stepped out, he courteously opened the door for Sarah. she asked curiously,

"Is the party at the Eiffel Tower?"

With a smile, Andrew replied, yes, my dear and led her to the top floor of the tower in an elevator. From there, they were greeted with a breathtaking view of the city, enhanced by pleasant weather and a gentle breeze that seemed to have left traces of recent rain.

Upon reaching the top floor, Sarah noticed that the area was completely dark. Suddenly, the lights came on, revealing a scene meticulously arranged by Andrew. He knelt before her, presenting a ring adorned with a beautifully crafted sapphire stone. The decorations were as per to Sarah's taste, with golden fairy lights illuminating the floor and rose petals adorning the table. Her favourite red wine awaited her, and the food had already been prepared according to her preferences. Andrew poured his heart out, expressing,

"Sarah, you have been my partner in crime, my best friend. You are the reason for my success, the one who constantly motivates me and sees the best in me. We have spent most of our lives as friends, but now, I wish to spend the rest of my life as your partner. Sarah, will you be mine forever?"

Overwhelmed, Sarah found herself in a state of turmoil. She said, "Andrew, please stand up. I have always cherished our friendship, but I don't envision a future together. I hope you understand. Friendship is something which I have always adored with you, I never want to lose such a great friend" With teary eyes, she hugged him.

Andrew, although heartbroken, concealed his emotions and responded, "It's your decision, and I respect that. I will always be your good friend."

Dark Side of the New Year

They proceeded with the dinner in an atmosphere of awkward silence before leaving the place. Not a single word was exchanged between them during the car ride. Meanwhile, Sarah pondered and spoke to herself, "Awe look at him, how cute he looks in the state of losing his love. I love him so much, but Andrew, I don't want to reveal my feelings until your birthday. So, my dear, wait for a couple of weeks." Their love remained pure and unspoken.

Andrew and Sarah were approaching Sarah's home, with Andrew driving at the allocated speed limit of approximately 50 km/h on that particular road. Unfortunately, one of the car's tires suddenly burst, causing the vehicle to collide with a traffic signal pole. Sarah, who wasn't wearing a seat belt, hit her head against the dashboard and lost consciousness. Meanwhile, Andrew was wearing his seat belt, and remained unharmed due to the speed limit regulations. Overwhelmed with panic upon seeing Sarah in this state, Andrew tried to revive her by sprinkling water on her face and gently shaking her, but to no avail. Realizing the severity of the situation, he promptly called for an ambulance to take her to the hospital. He left his car at the scene, which was later retrieved by his father.

Sarah was immediately rushed to the ICU upon arrival at the hospital, as her condition was critical. Andrew was entrusted with all of her belongings and was deeply shaken by the accident. While praying to God for Sarah's recovery, he received a call on Sarah's phone from her mother. His forehead was drenched in sweat as he anxiously contemplated on what to tell her. Initially, he decided not to answer the call. However, her mother persisted calling repeatedly; finally, on the fourth call, Andrew gathered the courage to pick up. Sarah's mother anxiously inquired, "Where are you? I'm worried about you. Why didn't you call to let me know you would be late?"

In a low and frightened voice, Andrew was struggling to speak through his tears. He managed to say, "Hi Aunt, it's Andrew. Sarah has been admitted to the hospital, and her condition is critical." Sarah's mother could only grasp the words "hospital" and "critical." Sensing the distress in Andrew's voice, she refrained from asking further questions and immediately asked to send the address and rushed to the hospital with Mr. Garcia. Within 15 minutes, they arrived at the hospital and approached the administrative staff, asking urgently, "Hello, has a patient named Sarah been admitted? She was brought here in a critical condition." The staff confirmed Sarah's admission to the ICU and informed them that the person who had been with her was waiting outside of the ICU.

Mr. and Mrs. Garcia briskly walked towards the ICU. They found Andrew in a state of distress, tears dripping down his face ceaselessly. Witnessing his condition, they became even more concerned. Mrs. Garcia couldn't hold back her

Dark Side of the New Year

tears and asked Andrew for an update on the situation. In response, he explained the details of the accident, expressing his uncertainty about Sarah's current condition as the doctors were still attending to her in the ICU. Together, they prayed for Sarah's well-being and speedy recovery.

Suddenly, the lights in the ICU dim, capturing everyone's attention as they anxiously turn their gaze towards the door. The doctors emerge, and a chorus of questions about Sarah's condition erupts from the concerned family. "Is she alright, doctor? Please tell us," They asks simultaneously. The doctor responds in a calm and composed manner, "Please everyone, calm down. She is currently out of danger, but she remains unconscious. We can only assess her health once she regains consciousness. For now, only one person can stay with her, while the others can visit in the morning. There are scheduled visiting hours from 11 a.m. to 3 p.m.". With these words, the doctor proceeds to look after other patients.

Mrs. Garcia asserts, "I want to be with my daughter. I'll take care of her." Mr. Garcia concurs saying, "Of course dear, you're the one who should be by her side. Andrew interjects into the conversation affirming, "Yes aunt, as a mother you can provide the best care for Sarah." Following their discussion, Andrew and Mr. Garcia leave the hospital, leaving Mrs. Garcia by Sarah's side.

At that moment, Sarah's mother sits beside her, determined to stay awake throughout the night. Lost in thoughts of her daughter's childhood, Mrs. Garcia reminisces about the times when Sarah would ask her to play hide-and-seek, drawing parallels between the game and the current situation. Speaking to Sarah, she says, "Sweetie, you are an indispensable part of my life and our family. How did this happen to you? Please stop playing hide-and-seek, just like you did in your childhood. Do you remember when we visited our farmhouse? You hid in the restroom on the first floor, and I searched for you everywhere but couldn't find you. I feel the same pain now but this time, you are lying in front of me and I am unable to wake you up. My hands are capable, yet they are powerless in this situation." Tears stream down her face as she hugs Sarah tightly. After pouring out her emotions, Mrs. Garcia goes silent, placing one hand on Sarah and she sleeps by her side. Watching her daughter intently, she eventually fell asleep.

In the morning, rays of sunlight gently illuminate Mrs. Garcia's and Sarah's faces. Mrs. Garcia awakens and gazes at her daughter, proclaiming, "Here lies the most beautiful daughter a mother could ask for." The sun's rays serve as a symbol of hope in their lives. Sarah gradually opens her eyes and utters, "Mom," tears streaming down her face incessantly. Mrs. Garcia's sorrowful expression transforms into sheer joy as her eyes well up with tears, witnessing this emotional moment. She embraces Sarah tightly.

Dark Side of the New Year

Mrs. Garcia hurries to the door, intending to call the doctor, and also contacts her husband, asks him to come to the hospital as soon as possible. Mr. Garcia reaches out to Andrew, for his presence at the hospital. When they arrive, they find Cathy engaged in a conversation with the doctor. Eager to know what transpired the event and why everyone appears so serious, they join the discussion. Cathy embraces her husband, and the doctor informs him that Sarah had opened her eyes. Unfortunately, she felt unconscious again after a few minutes due to fluctuating blood pressure. The doctor remains uncertain about when Sarah will regain consciousness. The doctor is called away by a nurse to attend to another patient.

Mr. Garcia embraces and consoles his wife saying, "Cathy, my dear, we need to stay strong. We must support our daughter." Although tears stream down his face, he conceals his emotions from her. Mr. and Mrs. Garcia approach the doctor once again and inquire whether they can take Sarah home, with a nurse visiting to monitor her condition. However, the doctor advises against it stating that it would be better for Sarah to remain in the hospital to receive immediate care in case of any emergency, as she is still in critical condition. The doctor assures them that once she is out of danger, they will consider granting permission. Mr. and Mrs. Garcia appears heartbroken by this response.

Meanwhile, Andrew arrives at the hospital and asks about Sarah's condition. Cathy impatiently, blames Andrew by saying, "It's all your fault that Sarah is in this state today. Why did you take her with you when you don't know how to drive properly?" Andrew is rendered speechless and simply apologizes to Mrs. Garcia. However, Mr. Garcia intervenes, calming his wife and stating, "Cathy, please calm down. It's not Andrew's fault. It was just an accident. I am upset with the situation as well, but we cannot blame him without any reason. Instead, we should be grateful that the car was under control, which is why Sarah is alive. Otherwise, we could have lost her. Also, it was Sarah's mistake for not wearing her seatbelt." Cathy apologizes to Andrew for her outburst, and he responds in a composed manner, saying, "Don't worry about it, I understand how Sarah's accident has affected us, and specially you Aunt."

Sarah's parents and Andrew consult the doctor, seeking guidance on how to handle the situation. They ask the doctor,

"What should we do from our end in this situation?"

The doctor advises them, "Please resume your routine lives. If you wish to visit Sarah, you can do so at any time. She will be under surveillance for at least a week."

Dark Side of the New Year

Mr. Garcia expresses gratitude saying, "Sure, thank you very much, doctor." They observe Sarah for a while before leaving the hospital.

Chapter 3
Nightmares

Once they arrive home, Andrew suggests, "I believe we should visit Sarah every day, turn by turn, so that she can be with her loved ones for a few hours at least." The couple agrees, saying, "That sounds like a good plan." Andrew suggests the visiting schedule, stating, "Mrs. Garcia will visit from 11 a.m. to 12:30 p.m., Mr. Garcia from 1 p.m. to 2 p.m., and I will visit between 3 p.m. and 5 p.m.." Mr. Garcia replies, "Fine. I have some work at the office, so I'll take your leave." Mr. Garcia runs his own publishing house, while Mrs.

Dark Side of the New Year

Garcia has a bakery that she started a year ago. She adds, "Yes, I also need to visit the bakery." Andrew says, "Even I should leave. I need to get back to the office." They begin visiting Sarah one by one according to their assigned time slots.

Andrew brings a bouquet for Sarah and places it on her bedside table. He also brings a glass flower pot, fills it with water, and transfers the flowers from the bouquet to the pot, hoping that the fragrance will reach Sarah and create a positive atmosphere in the ward. He sits beside her and apologizes, saying, "I'm sorry, Sarah. It's my fault that you're in this state of life. If I hadn't taken you to the Eiffel Tower to propose, everything could have been different. Why didn't I ask you to wear a seatbelt?" He remains by her side and discusses her condition with the doctor, asking,

"Sir, if there's anything I can do to improve Sarah's situation, please let me know."

The doctor responds, "The only thing you can do is to create a positive environment around her. Talk about happy moments with her and avoid discussing anything that may make her feel sad or hurt her emotions. Although she's currently unconscious, our observations suggest that she can hear what we say. In medical terms, it's referred to as a minor coma, where a patient may or may not respond to people speaking around them. A person can also respond through eye movements. Patients in a deep coma are unable to respond at all, but in Sarah's case, we can observe her eye movements. Therefore, please ensure that you help her maintain a positive mindset, which will contribute to her recovery."

Andrew assures the doctor, saying, "I will make sure to do that, and I will update Mr. and Mrs. Garcia to do the same."

After leaving the hospital, Andrew heads towards Sarah's home and informs her parents about the doctor's advice regarding her condition. He urges them to create a cheerful atmosphere whenever they are with her, and her parents readily agree. The following morning, when Mrs. Garcia visits the hospital, she brings colourful balloons and decorates Sarah's ward. Within half an hour, Mr. Garcia arrives with Andrew, carrying a variety of flowers and scented candles. They place the flowers on the side table and strategically arrange the candles throughout the room, lighting them one by one. They then sing a few lines for her, saying, "Just as sunlight illuminates the world, you bring light into our lives! You're the reason we continue to thrive in this world." They express their love for Sarah, and her eyes well up with tears of joy. Her eyes appear bright and filled with happiness.

Mr. Garcia starts recounting a story from Sarah's childhood, beginning with a laugh. He says, "Cathy, do you remember

Dark Side of the New Year

when we visited your father's place, and Sarah locked me on the balcony? She believed that I grew money on the money plant, and that's where her chocolates came from. Defiantly, she insisted that she would only open the door if I gave her money from the plant or bought her chocolates." Mrs. Garcia and Andrew laugh and Cathy replies "Yes Victor, I do remember. How could I forget that incident!" They continue reminiscing and sharing such anecdotes for about an hour.

At that moment, Andrew receives a call from his office. He responds, "Sure sir, I'll be there." After ending the call, he informs Mr. and Mrs. Garcia, "Uncle, aunt, I must take leave now. I need to be at the office. Please let me know if you need any help." With that, he leaves and makes his way to the office. Upon his arrival boss addresses him saying,

"Andrew, regarding the deal for which Sarah presented to the investors, they are willing to invest but they exclusively want to deal with Sarah. I have explained the situation to them, as you mentioned on the call, but it would be preferable if you could handle it."

Andrew assures his boss, "Certainly, sir. I will take care of it." He then proceeds to the meeting room to meet with the investors. Andrew explains,

"Gentlemen, I must inform you that Sarah is currently in critical condition and experiencing a minor coma. She is unable to communicate, but if you still wish to see her, we can arrange a visit to the hospital."

The investors respond, "Andrew, we understand the circumstances. It's not an issue. You will lead the project until Sarah recovers."

A week elapses following this routine where Cathy, Victor, and Andrew visit Sarah every day, endeavouring to bring her happiness. Then, on a remarkable day, Sarah's fingers reflected movement as she tries to converse with her mother expressing her love. Cathy becomes overwhelmed by the situation and summons the doctor to examine Sarah. The doctor affirms that Sarah is recovering, due to the positivity and joy they have instilled around her, which is commendable. However, the doctor advises against placing undue stress on Sarah or pressuring her to speak, allowing her to recover at her own pace. Cathy promptly calls her husband and Andrew to come to the hospital. Upon their arrival, they witness Sarah smiling and sharing a tender moment with her mother. Overwhelmed with joy, Andrew and Victor hugs each other. They enter the ward, where Cathy shares the doctor's words with them. Victor then approaches the doctor and inquires,

"Doctor, is it possible to discharge Sarah now, or does she still require further attention?"

Dark Side of the New Year

The doctor affirms, "Yes Mr. Victor, we can discharge Sarah at this point." Ecstatic and filled with happiness, they prepare the discharge paperwork, and the doctor arranges for a nurse to accompany them, ensuring that everything is set up and that Sarah receives the necessary care upon returning home.

They warmly welcome Sarah back into their home, where she is aided by a cane to assist her in walking. The nurse arranges her room with the necessary equipment in case of an emergency. Everyone gradually settles back into their daily routines, with the nurse present to care for Sarah. During dinner time, they assist Sarah in joining them at the dining table, ensuring she doesn't feel excluded. Her mother prepares all of her favourite dishes, one after another, on consecutive days to uplift her spirits. They enjoy watching entertainment or family movies together after dinner each night. Andrew continues to stay with them during this time.

A couple of days later, while everyone is asleep, Sarah unexpectedly screams around 2 a.m., calling out for her mom, dad, and Andrew. On seeing Sarah frightened her mother approaches her calmly, holding her hand and asking again what had happened. In a shaky voice, Sarah recounts, "A few minutes ago, I woke up to use the washroom with the help of the cane, not wanting to disturb any of you. But when I returned, I saw Michael standing in my room. Do you remember Andrew? I told you about the dream where he was trying to get closer to me. Well, that just happened now. Michael approached me, and as I was about to scream, he covered my mouth with his hand and forced me to sit on my bed. He held me around my waist and attempted to kiss me. I struck him with the cane and he fled as I screamed."

Everyone is filled with anger upon hearing about the incident. Andrew suggests to Victor, "Uncle, he can't have gone too far. Let's go after him." They rush downstairs in an attempt to find Michael, but their search proves futile. They even run to the main gate of their apartment, but he remains elusive. Victor advises Andrew that there's no use in continuing the search at this moment, we'll be lodging a complaint about Michael in the morning. They return home, and Victor suggests to his wife, Cathy,

"I think you should sleep with Sarah tonight as she is scared." He assures Sarah, "Don't worry, my love. We will file a complaint against him in the morning."

However, Sarah replies, "No, Dad, we won't be doing that."

Perplexed, Victor asks her for a reason, but she simply responds with a firm "No." The nurse intervenes, requesting Victor not to force Sarah, considering she has recently faced a dangerous situation. Victor agrees, acknowledging the nurse's point, and says to Sarah,

Dark Side of the New Year

"Alright, I suppose you're right." They leave the room, allowing Sarah to rest.

Days and weeks passed; Sarah continued to face sleepless nights due to the traumatic incident involving Michael. Each day, she would attempt to walk with the support of a cane, but unfortunately, her efforts were in vain. However, on a sunny day, she woke up and determinedly made another attempt, this time successfully navigating a slow walk until she reached the hallway. The sight filled everyone with joy, witnessing Sarah's independent steps. Sarah exclaimed, "Look, I'm walking on my own!" During the excitement, she momentarily neglected her well-being, resulting in her leg slipping on the carpet. Thankfully, Andrew quickly reacted, catching her and preventing a fall. Concerned, all three of them urged Sarah, "Please take care of yourself, Sarah."

Victor immediately contacted the doctor to inform him about Sarah's achievement in walking. The doctor responded, "Whenever she walks, ensure that a nurse or someone else is present with her. She still requires attention and care. However, it's truly remarkable to see her rapid recovery." Victor expressed his gratitude, saying, "Thank you, doctor!" Victor relayed the doctor's advice to Sarah, informing her, "The doctor mentioned that you shouldn't walk alone." He then addressed the nurse, saying, "Please stay by her side at all times and ensure she doesn't slip while walking." The nurse nodded and replied, "sure, Mr. Garcia."

After a month, life had returned to normalcy for Sarah. She regained her ability to walk independently, and the nurse was no longer needed Andrew had also returned to his home. Sarah was excited to resume her work at the office. On her first day back, she was warmly welcomed and greeted by her colleagues and boss.

The boss informed Sarah that the deal with the investors had been finalized. Due to her absence, Andrew took charge of the project. The boss informed Sarah that she could join Andrew in working on the project. Sarah replied, "sure, sir." Andrew and Sarah began working together on the project, with Andrew overseeing the procurement of materials.

However, on a particular day, their boss entered the room and noticed Sarah looking upset with tears streaming down her face. In a concerned tone he asked Sarah, "What happened, are you alright?" Sarah explained that as an experienced assistant buyer in the company, she wanted to source materials from an old merchant. Whereas Andrew preferred a new one that he had found. This disagreement had escalated into a heated argument, during which Andrew had allegedly slapped me for not following his orders as he is the project head.

The boss was visibly displeased with Andrew's behaviour and admonished him, saying, "Andrew, this is not what I expected from someone like you." Andrew calmly and respectfully denied the accusation, stating that it was just an

Dark Side of the New Year

argument and I didn't slap Sarah, I'm in love with her how can I do it to her. Despite Andrew's denial, the boss issued him a warning, stating that it was his first and last warning. The boss made it clear that any recurrence of such incidents would result in Andrew being fired, urging him to be cautious of his actions.

Andrew found himself taken aback by Sarah's behaviour and became lost in his thoughts. He contemplated that perhaps Sarah had not fully recovered and also, she may be upset regarding the proposal and the accident. Moreover, their argument further strained their relationship. Lost in his thoughts, Andrew silently reflected on the situation.

Finally, he gathered himself and told Sarah, "It's alright if you prefer to proceed with the old merchant. I understand." Sarah's face brightened with happiness and she responded, "Thank you, Andrew. I appreciate it." Determined to make things right, Sarah decided to leave and purchase the materials.

After a few hours, Sarah called Andrew to convey a change in plans. She expressed her desire not to proceed with the old merchant and requested Andrew contact his preferred merchant instead. With those words, she abruptly ended the call. Sarah arrived at the office later, prompting Andrew to inquire about the sudden change. He asked, "Sarah, what happened? Why did you cancel the order when you were so keen on working with the old merchant?" Sarah proceeded to explain her decision, revealing that the materials offered by the old merchant did not meet their brand's reputation. Andrew accepted her explanation and assured her, "Alright, I have already contacted my merchant. We can explore the materials they are offering."

To demonstrate the alternative materials, Andrew brought a few samples to the office and presented them to Sarah. She carefully examined them and expressed her satisfaction, stating, "The materials are of high quality, and the fabric is suitable for our needs. We can proceed with them." After finalizing the materials, Andrew proposed, "Sarah, would you like to go out for dinner tonight?" Sarah's face lit up with a smile as she happily replied, "Sure, why not? I'd love to."

They arrived at Sarah's favourite restaurant, only to unexpectedly encounter the doctor who had treated her. Andrew and Sarah greeted the doctor, and he introduced his wife, Emma. Andrew suggested, "Why don't we all dine together?" Both the doctor and his wife agreed, and he added, "Please feel free to call me Marc, and this is my wife, Emma." Andrew smiled, and replies, sure.

They all gathered around the table, preparing to enjoy their meal. Marc attentively observed Sarah, ensuring she was doing well. Suddenly, he excused himself, stating, "Excuse me, everyone. I'll be right back." Marc left for a few minutes, tending to an urgent matter.

Dark Side of the New Year

In the meantime, Sarah said, excuse me guys, I'll be back. She approached the cash counter, engaged in a brief conversation with the manager, and swiftly returned to the table. Sarah informed every one about the situation by saying, "The head chef is on leave today, and the restaurant is managing with their regular chef staff. Considering the circumstances, I don't think it would be the best option to dine here. Shall we find another restaurant for dinner?" Andrew agreed, responding, "That sounds reasonable. Marc and Emma, are you both okay with changing venues?" to which they replied, "Certainly, we don't see any problem with that."

They proceeded to a nearby restaurant, where they enjoyed their dinner and eventually departed from there, greeting each other.

The next day, Marc contacted Andrew and requested a meeting at the hospital at 11 a.m. Andrew was lost in the thoughts about the reason Marc contacted him. He arrived at Marc's office and inquired about the purpose of the meeting. Marc gestured for him to take a seat and began the conversation. He asked Andrew if he had noticed any unusual changes in Sarah's behaviour or the things she said. Andrew confirmed, saying,

"Yes, I've been thinking about it since yesterday morning."

Dark Side of the New Year

Intrigued, Marc asked Andrew to elaborate on the morning incident. Andrew proceeded to explain what had transpired in the office, how Sarah had argued about purchasing materials from the old merchant and falsely accused Andrew of slapping her. However, she later changed her stance, opting to buy from Andrew's preferred merchant due to concerns about fabric quality. Andrew expressed his astonishment at how quickly Sarah's behaviour had changed. Marc says, that's quite unusual. Here, Andrew interrupts and says, to investigate further, I decided to visit the old merchant without informing anyone and discovered that nothing unusual had occurred. Sarah had merely looked at the materials and stated she would return the following day. I had taken the new stock from the same place, showing it to Sarah. Surprisingly, she responded positively and suggested proceeding with the same merchant.

Marc seized upon this revelation and mentioned an incident from the previous day at the restaurant. He recounted how he had overheard Sarah conversing with the restaurant manager, claiming that she enjoyed the food and the atmosphere they had created but nothing about head chef. Marc expressed his confusion and curiosity, asking Andrew if he recalled any other recent incidents similar to these. Andrew pondered for a few moments and recollected the night when Sarah had screamed and informed everyone about a man named Michael being present in her room, attempting to harm her. Andrew revealed that Michael was

Dark Side of the New Year

her cab driver on New Year's Eve. Perplexed by these revelations, Marc concluded that he needed to discuss the matter with Sarah in a more light hearted manner. He requested Andrew to arrange another dinner at the same restaurant for that evening. Andrew agreed, saying, "Sure, I will take care of it," and left Marc's office to make the necessary arrangements.

In the evening, they reconvened at the same restaurant where Sarah had previously mentioned the head chef's absence. Sarah expressed her enjoyment of the dinner to Andrew and Marc, remarking on the deliciousness of the food. She asserted that if they had dined there the previous day, they wouldn't have savoured it as much due to the chef's absence. Andrew and Marc agreed with her, acknowledging the good food quality. They decided to summon the manager to convey their appreciation. The manager arrived, and Marc complimented the delectable food, praising the commendable service. Marc also mentioned that they had considered visiting the restaurant the previous day but refrained upon hearing about the chef's absence. To their surprise, the manager responded with a puzzled expression, stating that, the chef had indeed been working on that day, there was a late-night party yesterday, making it impossible for the chef to be on leave. Sarah interjected calmly, affirming her previous conversation with the manager regarding the chef's absence. However, the manager politely contradicted her, stating that their conversation had solely revolved around the restaurant being her favourite. The manager leaves from there saying thank you.

Perplexed, Sarah expressed her shock and questioned why the manager would lie. Marc observed Sarah's reaction and inquired if such incidents frequently occurred around her. Sarah, with a bewildered expression, confirmed that similar occurrences had taken place. She recounted how Andrew had slapped her during an argument in the office, but he had denied it when confronted by their boss. Marc probed further, asking if anything else had troubled her over the past month. Sarah disclosed the unsettling incident of encountering Michael in her room at 2 a.m., where he had attempted to approach her physically. She explained that she had screamed, and when others arrived, Michael had fled. Marc asked if she had experienced similar scenarios before, such as being slapped in her dreams or colleagues being on leave. Sarah reflected for a moment and recalled a vivid dream from a few months ago, where her best friend accidentally slapped her while playing basketball when they were both 13 years old. She also mentioned a recent dream in which her boss was on leave, and she had to handle her workload as well as that of the other staff. Marc concluded that Sarah had been under considerable stress and offered her some medication to alleviate her concerns. He suggested leaving the restaurant, and they departed. However, Marc discreetly texted Andrew, requesting him and Sarah's parents to visit the hospital at 10 a.m. the following day.

Chapter 4
Fabricated Stories

On the appointed day, Andrew, Cathy, and Victor arrived at the hospital to meet with Marc. They inquired about the reason behind the meeting and sought an explanation from the doctor. Marc urged Cathy and Victor to pay close attention and handle the situation with great care. He proceeded to recount the entire story, starting with both dinners and the meeting he had with Andrew. Marc revealed that Sarah's actions were interconnected with her dreams, suggesting that she was experiencing hallucinations and fabricating events based on her convenience. This was a medical condition that required delicate handling. He cautioned that if they were to confront Sarah directly about the situation, she might faint or invent fabricated stories.

As her parents and friend, he urged them not to automatically believe everything she said, as it may not be grounded in reality. Marc recommended they speak with Michael to verify whether he had visited their house or not. He believed that Sarah's propensity for fabrication was a result of her accident and head injury. He further explained that Sarah hadn't been in a coma for an extended period, but when she woke up and called out for her mother initially, she was unconscious again. In reality, she had been conscious but dreams prevented her from responding to their words. Although all her medical tests indicated normal functioning, Marc had refrained from allowing her to be discharged immediately, and the presence of the nurse was to monitor her closely. He emphasized that the nurse had been awake throughout the entire night, sitting in the room, yet Sarah hadn't even noticed her. Marc concluded that Michael had never entered Sarah's room and that the entire story had been concocted within her imagination.

Cathy and Victor appeared concerned upon hearing the news. Marc reassured them, urging them to remain calm and avoid stress. He explained that with the proper medication, Sarah's condition could be treated, gradually reducing the intensity and frequency of her hallucinations. He emphasized that it was fortunate that they had identified the issue at an early stage, as it would have been more challenging to address it without medication. Marc stressed the importance of ensuring that Sarah receives sufficient sleep in a calm and happy environment. He encouraged Cathy and Victor to be a source of strength for Sarah during this time. Andrew expressed his gratitude to Marc for his assistance and assured Mr. and Mrs. Garcia that he would do his utmost to support Sarah. Marc handed Andrew a prescription for the necessary medicines, instructing him to give it three times a day without fail to Sarah. After thanking the doctor, they left the hospital, purchased the prescribed medicines, and began Sarah's treatment confidentially. Cathy prepared the medication by mixing the powdered form with water and administering it to Sarah without her knowledge.

A few days later, Sarah awoke from her sleep with heavy and tense breathing. She proceeded to the kitchen to fetch some water. However, to her surprise, she overheard Andrew's voice coming from her parents' room. Intrigued, she pressed her ear against the door, hoping to catch their conversation. Inside, she heard Cathy assuring Victor that she was administering Sarah's medication, fully aware of the dangers posed by her hallucinations. Sarah's face remained expressionless upon hearing about her condition, as if all joy had been drained from her life. She slowly made her way back to her room, consumed by thoughts of her childhood best friend, Jean. Despite being a lawyer by profession, Jean possessed an inherent curiosity that could have made her an exceptional detective. However, her true passion lay in the field of law.

Sarah immediately dialled Jean's number, talking to herself in a tearful voice, determined not to take any chances of succumbing to hallucinations again. She expressed her doubts about her ability to distinguish the truth from the stories she might fabricate. Upon answering the call, Jean provided comfort to Sarah, encouraging her to calm down and share her troubles. Sarah proceeded to explain the entire situation regarding her hallucinations, including a recent dream that felt distinct from the others—a dream where she was referred to as Sofia and responded to that name. This particular dream had jolted her awake, leaving her breathless and desperate for Jean's assistance. In response, Jean offered words of solace, advising Sarah to remain calm and scheduling a meeting for the following day at 10 a.m. in her office. Grateful for Jean's support, Sarah mustered a feeble "Thank you, my saviour" before ending the call.

The following day, Sarah met Jean at her office, and they delved into a comprehensive discussion about the sequence of events, starting from Sarah's encounter with Michael on new year to the dream where she was called Sofia. Jean advised Sarah to remain vigilant to any suspicious activities and asked Sarah to contact her promptly if anything seemed amiss. Grateful for Jean's guidance, Sarah assured her that she would be attentive and thanked her for the support.

Meanwhile, Andrew contacted Nancy, inquiring about her mother's condition and expressing his hopes for her recovery. Nancy responded with a sombre tone, indicating that there had been no improvement. She added that she and her father had grown accustomed to the situation. Andrew apologized for his absence from visiting their home over the past few weeks but assured Nancy that he had a valid reason, which he would disclose when they met. He requested her location, intending to join her. Nancy informed him that she was currently at her office and suggested meeting at the nearby coffee shop. Andrew agreed, promising to arrive within half an hour.

Nancy waited at the coffee shop until Andrew's arrival. Upon seeing him, she embraced him warmly and inquired about his well-being. Andrew responded positively, suggesting that they order something to drink. They both ordered coffee, settling into a conversation. Nancy asked Andrew to explain his recent behaviour. Andrew proceeded to share the details with her, recounting the proposal and the subsequent involvement with Sarah's medication. Nancy appeared deeply concerned upon hearing about Sarah's situation, exclaiming,

Dark Side of the New Year

"Oh my God! Andrew, why didn't you tell me anything before? You both were going through so much, and I would have done whatever was within my power to help. You should have informed me."

Andrew apologized, acknowledging that he had unintentionally neglected to inform her, particularly considering the challenges she was facing in her own life while caring for her mother and managing her work. Nancy expressed her desire to meet Sarah immediately, suggesting they go together. Andrew agreed, and the two of them headed towards Sarah's office.

As Nancy entered Sarah's office, Sarah approached her, embracing her warmly and inquiring about her well-being and her mother's condition. Nancy replied that she was fine, but there had been no improvement in her mother's health. Sarah apologized for her inability to visit Nancy's home earlier due to her circumstances but promised to make time to visit her mother that day. Nancy responded with a comforting tone, assuring Sarah that it was understandable and mentioning that Andrew had already informed her about the situation. She expressed regret for not being there for Sarah during her time of need. However, Nancy invited both Andrew and Sarah to her home later that day, as it was her mother's birthday, and they had planned a celebration to create a joyful atmosphere for her. Nancy revealed that they had invited her mother's friends and family members, hoping that seeing their loved ones would bring her happiness. Sarah enthusiastically replied, promising to arrive by 5 pm. Andrew said, we would be by the clock. Nancy asked for the leave as she had some pending tasks to attend to. Andrew and Sarah bid her goodbye and agreed to meet later.

Sarah suggested to Andrew that they buy a gift for Mrs. Bernard and leave the office by 3 p.m. Andrew agreed, acknowledging it as a good idea, and they both focused on completing their work by the specified time. As they were engrossed in their tasks, Sarah's phone emitted a beep, indicating that it was 3 p.m. Sarah notified Andrew, asking if they should leave. He responded with a smile, remarking on Sarah's foresight in setting the alarm for their departure. Sarah said, "It was indeed important". Andrew suggested that they could shop at Eastfield Forum des Hales. Sarah agreed, recognizing it as a great shopping destination. They arrived at the location, and Sarah surveyed the surroundings, pointing out a gift store that caught her attention. She expressed her belief that they should visit the store, describing it as appealing. They explored the store, searching for appropriate gifts, but Sarah expressed her disappointment in not finding anything suitable. However, her eyes landed on a laughing Buddha statue, and she approached it, suggesting that they gift it along with Mrs.

Dark Side of the New Year

Bernard's favourite French perfume. Andrew agreed, approving of the idea. They purchased gifts and a bouquet.

By 5 p.m., they had arrived at the Bernard residence, where Sarah had invited Jean, who was already present. Jean and Nancy were good friends through their connection with Sarah. Sarah and Andrew were greeted by Mr. Bernard at the door, and they entered the room to meet Mrs. Bernard. They placed the bouquet and Buddha statue on the side table and applied some perfume to Mrs. Bernard's hand and neck, allowing her to enjoy the fragrance. Once all the guests had arrived, everyone gathered in Mehak's room. Mr. Bernard brought in the cake with excitement, placing it on the table. They all sang the happy birthday song and clapped while Andrew played the guitar in the background, knowing Mehak's fondness for music. Both father and daughter cut the cake together on behalf of Mehak and shared it with everyone. Mr. Bernard invited everyone to relax and enjoy themselves, mentioning that dinner was also ready. They engaged in various games and activities. During this time, Andrew received a call and stepped out of the main door to answer it. He spoke to his friend, confessing that he was with Sarah only for her wealth, as he wouldn't chose to be with a girl who hallucinates and fabricates stories. He admitted that it was not what he truly desired, but he saw an opportunity to benefit financially from her affluent family, which motivated him to try to convince her to marry him.

Suddenly, someone tugged at Andrew from behind, causing him to turn around. To his surprise, it was Sarah. He called out her name, but she responded by slapping him and storming off in tears, leaving the party. Sarah spoke to herself in her thoughts, expressing her disbelief at how someone could be so heartless. Jean attempted to find Sarah at the party but was unable to find her. However, she couldn't leave the party as Nancy prevented her from doing so.

Dark Side of the New Year

Chapter 5
A Secret Revelation

Sarah hailed a cab and directed the driver to take her home. On the way, she noticed the Eiffel Tower and requested the driver to stop there, paying the fare accordingly. The driver called out to her, informing her about the change she was owed. However, Sarah proceeded forward without looking back. She found a spot near the river Seine and sat there, devoid of expression, tears streaming down her face. Thoughts of Andrew consumed her mind, questioning how he could betray her like this. Coincidentally, Michael, who was driving his taxi along the same path, noticed Sarah crying. He stopped the car, approached her and took a seat beside her. Concerned, he asked why she was alone and in tears, inquiring if something was amiss. Sarah hugged him and wept uncontrollably. Michael provided comfort and urged her to confide in him, assuring her that he would do his best to help. Sarah proceeded to explain everything that had transpired with Andrew and what she had overheard. Michael expressed his anger towards Andrew for breaking Sarah's heart and reassured her that they would find a way to teach him a lesson.

Feeling a sense of relief, Sarah pondered why she had trusted Michael so implicitly since the day they met, even though she had no prior knowledge of him before the new year. She expressed gratitude to Michael for his comforting words, acknowledging that he had made her feel better. Michael made her comfortable but she couldn't understand the logic behind why he appeared in her dream, where he was trying to misbehave with her. Doubts crept in as she wondered if she had done something wrong. Overwhelmed, she pleaded for divine intervention, seeking salvation from her turmoil.

Michael suggested that he will drop her home so she could rest. He emphasized the importance of taking her medication on time during this stage of her life. He offered her his contact number, assuring her that she could reach out whenever she needed someone to talk to or if she required any form of assistance within his capability. Sarah expressed her gratitude for his kind gesture and requested that he also note down her number. They departed from the location, and Michael dropped Sarah back to her home.

To Sarah's surprise, she discovered Andrew waiting for her at the main entrance of her house. Filled with anger, she confronted him exclaiming,

"Andrew, what are you doing here? Why are you even here? Just get lost from my home and my life. I never want to see you again. I always believed you truly loved me, but you turned out to be a greedy person. I considered you my friend and started loving you, you are nothing but pathetic. I hate you!"

Andrew requested Sarah to calm down, professing his love for her and insisting that he had orchestrated the plan to make her realize her true feelings. He claimed to have noticed her following him at the party and devised a scheme to provoke her by pretending to be on a call. According to Andrew, his plan had succeeded, as Sarah had just confessed her love for him. Sarah vehemently denied Andrew's interpretation, stating,

Dark Side of the New Year

"No, Andrew, I don't trust you anymore. The method you implemented was cliché and insincere. Please leave right now."

Andrew apologized profusely, begging for forgiveness and promising that he would never hurt her. He professed his unwavering love for her, willing to do anything for her sake. As Sarah's anger intensified, Andrew recognized the futility of his efforts and departed when he noticed her face turning red with rage. Sarah entered her home and embraced her mother, but she refrained from revealing her about the hallucinations. Without any argument, she silently accepted the water offered by her mother and went to her bed to sleep.

The following morning, Sarah noticed multiple missed calls from Jean on her phone. She promptly returned the call and inquired about the reason for Jean's urgency. Jean questioned her about the events of the previous night's party and her absence. Sarah recounted the entire story, venting her frustrations about Andrew's despicable behaviour. Jean advised her to be cautious and mindfulness in response to everything happening around her. Jean suggested that Sarah feign love for Andrew, making him believe that you trust him and accepted his words from the previous night. However, she cautioned Sarah to remain vigilant, using this act as an opportunity to investigate

Andrew and his family, aiming to uncover the true reasons behind his behaviour. Sarah expressed doubt about her ability to carry out such a plan but agreed to give it a try. She expressed her gratitude to Jean, acknowledging the invaluable support and assistance she had provided during this challenging period of her life. Jean replied, reassuring Sarah that she would always be there for her as her best friend, emphasizing that it was her duty as a friend. They both said bye, concluding their conversation.

Sarah's parents contacted Andrew as he had been visiting them daily, but he failed to show up on that particular day. They called out to him, asking where he was and if he could come over. Andrew responded, "Okay, uncle, I'll be there in an hour." Cathy informed Sarah that Andrew would be arriving shortly. Sarah acknowledged her mother's message with a simple "Fine, Mom," and proceeded to get dressed. Following Jean's advice, Sarah prepared herself for the upcoming encounter. As soon as Andrew arrived, Sarah greeted him cheerfully, saying,

"Hey, Andrew, nice to see you."

His bewildered expression indicated surprise at Sarah's changed behaviour. Sarah suggested they sit in her room, to which Andrew responded, "Sure, dear, why not." Seated in her room, Sarah confessed to Andrew that she had become aware of her hallucinations. She revealed that she overheard a conversation between him and her mother a

Dark Side of the New Year

few days ago when she woke up in the middle of the night. Sarah explained that she dreamt of Andrew loving her solely for her money and inquired if he had discussed such matters the previous night. Andrew reassured her, denying any such conversation had taken place. Sarah apologized, admitting that she had shouted at him without any reason. She then acted as though her suspicions were merely products of her hallucinations, successfully convincing Andrew. Sarah expressed her love for Andrew, apologizing for the delay in recognizing her feelings. Andrew embraced her and replied,

"Don't worry, Sarah. It sometimes takes time for a person to understand their own emotions. Let's celebrate our love today! I'll book a banquet hall for this evening and invite all our friends and family for 7 p.m."

Guests started arriving at the party at 7 p.m.. The venue was arranged like a club, offering a sophisticated atmosphere suitable for a family dinner. Everyone thoroughly enjoyed the festivities, dancing together and revelling in the joyous atmosphere. Sarah and Andrew showcased a mesmerizing dance performance that left the guests in awe, capturing their attention entirely. Inspired by their performance, the other couples joined them on stage to dance together. Simultaneously, a delicious spread of food was prepared for the guests. Meanwhile, Jean keenly observed the party, attempting to uncover any connections to Sarah's life.

She had a conversation with Mr. Bernard, asking about Mehak aunt's health. Mr. Bernard sadly informed her that Mehak's condition remained unchanged. Jean expressed her concern, inquiring about the circumstances surrounding the incident and who was with her at that time. Mr. Bernard shared his surprise, recounting how he couldn't find Mehak in the house and eventually discovered her on the terrace. Initially thinking she was enjoying the weather, he approached her but then noticed she had fell from the terrace. Hurriedly looking over the edge, he found her lying on the ground. He immediately rushed her to the hospital, where she was diagnosed with paralysis. Jean expressed her sympathy, apologizing for the situation. Mr. Bernard assured her that he and Nancy are habituated with the situation and encouraged her to enjoy the party. As the evening progressed, the guests enjoyed their dinner, and the party concluded around 11:30 p.m. Guests placed their cards and gifts on the designated tables before bidding farewell to the party.

Jean meticulously trails Mr. Bernard's every move, patiently waiting in her car at his apartment's parking area. Around 1 a.m., she notices him leaving his home, raising her suspicions. Intrigued, Jean decides to follow him. She observes Mr. Bernard heading towards a nearby chemist store and returning with a brown package before making his way back home. Puzzled by his late-night errand, Jean contemplates the situation from her parked car and ponders

Dark Side of the New Year

why he didn't buy the medicine during the morning. Eventually, Jean returns to her place.

After the party, Andrew asks Sarah if they can go on a long drive. Sarah agrees, and he drops her off at around 1:30 a.m. before driving away. However, upon hearing the sound of his car departing, Sarah's curiosity gets the better of her, and she decides to follow Andrew in her car. She notices that Andrew takes a different route than the one to his area, sparking suspicion within Sarah that he might be involved in some sort of drug operation. Andrew parks his car and enters a building using the elevator. Sarah parks her car at a distance and observes the elevator stopping on the third floor. In this situation, she decides to use the staircase and conceals herself on the second-floor landing.

After half an hour, Andrew reemerges and opens the door with a creaking voice, prompting Sarah to peer through the stairs. She spots a woman standing at the doorstep who mentions meeting Andrew at their favourite coffee shop at 5 p.m. the next day. Andrew agrees and says her goodnight before leaving. Sarah discreetly captures a picture of the lady. She continues to follow Andrew, but this time he heads back to his own home, causing Sarah to return to her residence.

The next day, Sarah visits Jean's office and recounts the events of the previous day, showing her the picture of the mysterious woman. They attempt to find her on Andrew's social media profiles but are unsuccessful. They decide to keep an eye on Andrew and follow him to the coffee shop in the evening. Jean instructs Sarah to go to the office and monitor Andrew's activities. Surprisingly, Sarah finds Andrew in the office and asks him with surprise,

"What are you doing here, Andrew? You never come to the office early. Are you alright?"

Andrew responds, "Yes, Sarah, I'm perfectly fine. I just have a lot of pending work and looming project deadlines to meet. Apart from that, I have a meeting scheduled for this evening."

Sarah enquires about the meeting, and Andrew apologizes, explaining that it's personal and he cannot disclose the details. Sarah understandingly replies,

"No problem. Let's focus on the project. We need to finalize the designs today and send them for stitching." Both Sarah and Andrew then immersed themselves in their work.

In the meantime, Bernard left his house, feeling as though someone was following him in a car with tinted windows. He notices the other car make a right turn, causing Mr Bernard to question his initial suspicion. Mr Bernard proceeds on his way. He arrives at a peculiar and desolate warehouse, seemingly untouched for a long time. He waits in his car at the location for approximately 10 minutes before stepping out. A woman joined him and someone took a photo of their interaction without their knowledge. They talked for about 30 minutes, hugged, and left separately, just as they had arrived. Mr Bernard heads back home, unaware that the same car continues to tail him. After arriving at his home, he climbs up the stairs while the other car was parked in the lot for the whole night. Mr Bernard attends to his wife's care.

Meanwhile, Andrew informs Sarah, "Hey, I'm heading to the meeting I mentioned earlier. It's something special for you. I'll let you know the details soon." Sarah responds with a wide smile, expressing her excitement and fondness for surprises. However, deep down, she contemplates Andrew's ulterior motives, fully aware of his capability to manipulate situations. Sarah thinks, "Let's see what game you're playing with me now, Andrew." Andrew embraces Sarah, but she reacts by slapping him, expressing her displeasure at his inappropriate behaviour. Sarah confronts Andrew, saying,

"How dare you pull my dress!"

Andrew calmly denies any wrongdoing, stating that he simply hugged her. Sarah becomes even more furious, demanding Andrew to leave her alone. Andrew responds politely,

"I'm sorry if you feel that way," and exits the office, assuming it may be another episode of Sarah's hallucinations.

Dark Side of the New Year

Sarah's facial expression reveals that it was not a hallucination. She internally muses, "Andrew, you have issues with my hallucinations, but let me show you the extent to which they can do." Sarah changes into different attire, conceals her face with a scarf, and wears goggles. In the coffee shop, she sits behind Andrew, facing the opposite direction, to ensure they remain unaware of her presence. Sarah overhears their conversation, which does not reveal anything suspicious. They simply discuss their respective work and prepare to leave. However, Andrew's remarks leave Sarah surprised. After they depart, Sarah hastily returns to her office before Andrew arrives. She immerses herself in her pending design work. When Andrew eventually arrives, they discuss the project's progress, finalizing designs for half of the required slots.

Later, Sarah contacts Jean and shares an astonishing revelation, saying,

"Jean, you won't believe what I just found out. I'm still in shock."

Curious, Jean inquires, "What happened? What's troubling you?"

Sarah responds with a fearful and surprised tone, "That lady we saw, she's Andrew's mother!"

Dark Side of the New Year

Perplexed, Jean exclaims, "Sarah, how is that possible? And if it's true, why are they both hiding from the world?"

Sarah, still trying to process the information, speculates, "I don't know what's going on. I suspect Andrew's mother might be involved in illegal activities. And could be the reason for their secrecy."

Jean advises Sarah to wait for a suitable moment to casually bring it up without seeming too intrusive. Jean emphasizes the importance of choosing her words carefully. Sarah agrees, assuring Jean that she will be cautious, and ends the call. Andrew and Sarah leave the office and head towards their respective homes

Chapter 6
The Long-Lost Truth

Meanwhile, Jean visits the Bernard residence to meet Mehak. While conversing, Jean voices her doubts about Mr. Bernard, which leads to Mehak's blood pressure rising up. Concerned, Mehak calls for the nurse who is present in their home to administer an injection. The nurse tells Jean to avoid stressful topics when talking to Mehak and focus on happy things. Jean notices that Mehak's eyes fill with anger at the mention of Mr. Bernard's name, but she still complies. Jean is determined to understand the situation and asks if

Dark Side of the New Year

there is an issue with Mr. Bernard. Mehak responds positively with her eyes, indicating that the problem is not related to Sarah but Mr. Bernard Jean probes further, asking if the problem involves Mehak herself. Mehak confirms with a yes. As Jean is intrigued by the revelation, she continues to question as she is concerned for Nancy.

Just then, Mr. Bernard arrives at the house, greeting Jean and asking how she is doing. She replies him, stating that everything is fine and she simply wants to check on Mehak's health. Mr. Bernard appreciates her thoughtfulness and suggests they have a cup of coffee. As they make their way to the kitchen, he prepares coffee while Jean offers her assistance. Accidentally, Jean drops his wallet that is resting on the kitchen counter. Apologizing, she bends down to pick it and she notices Mehak's picture in the wallet. However, as she takes a closer look, another photo slips out from behind, revealing the name "Lucie" on it. Jean discreetly returns the wallet without asking any questions and apologizes once again. Mr. Bernard assures her that it's not a problem. They enjoy their coffee together, and when Jean departs from the house, she sits in her car, visibly tensed and worried. Her breathing becomes heavy, and she drinks water to calm herself down before leaving the premises for the time being.

The next day, Sarah and Andrew resume their work on the project as usual. At the same time, Jean works diligently to understand the events by organizing them into a logical sequence. In the evening, Sarah returns from her office but encounters a problem with her car. It breaks down, emitting smoke from the engine. Stepping out of the vehicle, she lifts the bonnet to inspect the damage. In need of a lift or a taxi, a cab conveniently pulls over, and to her surprise, it's Michael behind the wheel. Sarah greets him, saying, "Oh, hi, Michael. Can you give me a ride to home? My car's engine is damaged, and I may need to call for a tow truck."

"Sure, come on in, Sarah," Michael agrees.

During their ride, Sarah and Michael discussed their recent meeting. They focused on Sarah's decision to forgive Andrew for past events and how they are now back together.

In a state of shock, Michael abruptly stops the car, questioning Sarah,

"What happened, Sarah? How did you trust him again? And why?"

Sarah responds, mentioning Michael's name, then fainting suddenly.

Worried about her condition, Michael tries to awake her, sprinkling water on her face and attempting to wake her up, but she remains unresponsive. Fortunately, Michael's home

Dark Side of the New Year

is nearby, so he decides to take Sarah there. She rests for a while, while Michael contacts a doctor, requesting a house visit for his patient. However, due to emergency cases at the hospital, the doctor apologizes and informs Michael that a visit is not possible. Instead, the doctor provides instructions for remedies that can be followed. Michael expresses his gratitude and assures the doctor that he will adhere to the advice. Following the doctor's instructions, Michael prepares a mixture of medicine with water and administers it to Sarah, waiting patiently for her to regain consciousness. In the meantime, he starts preparing dinner.

Sarah gradually wakes up, her eyes scanning the unfamiliar surroundings. She sees Michael and inquires,

"Where are we, Michael?"

He responds, "We're at my home. You fainted in the car during our conversation, and since my house was nearby, I brought you here to rest. I also gave you the prescribed medicine from the doctor."

Sarah expresses her gratitude, saying, "Thank you, Michael. It means a lot to me."

Michael replies, "It was my duty, Sarah. I consider you a friend, and I believe it's my responsibility to fulfil the duties of a friend. You will have dinner here tonight."

Sarah initially declines, insisting on returning home.

However, Michael insists on at least having some snacks, stating that since she's visiting his home for the first time, she should eat something.

Sarah laughs and relents, saying, "Alright, Michael."

Michael prepares noodles for both of them. While eating, Sarah notices a photograph placed on a side table. She panics and questions Michael,

"How do you have this picture?"

Michael explains, "Sarah, remember when I told you about my wife's accident and my daughter being taken away from me? Well, they are my wife and daughter."

Upon hearing this, Sarah drops the plate from her trembling hands.

Michael anxiously asks, "What happened, Sarah?"

Overwhelmed with mixed emotions, Sarah begins to cry and says, "Michael, that's me in the picture! It's my childhood photo! I can show you a picture of the same age with my parents on my phone."

Dark Side of the New Year

She proceeds to show him the picture, and Michael is astonished, exclaiming, "That's my cousin and his wife! I can't believe they were the ones who separated me from you."

Sarah embraces Michael and says, "You're my real father, and I had no idea! Once I get home, I will inquire about why I was kept in the dark."

Michael advises Sarah not to mention anything to Victor and Cathy, to which she agrees, saying, "Alright, Dad. I won't. But why didn't you try to find me?"

Michael responds, "I did try, my dear. However, after six months, I was told that you had been in an accident with your guardians and were no longer alive." He continues, "Now, dear, you should return home. Cathy and Victor may be worrying about you." Michael drives her back home and says, "We will meet tomorrow at my place." Sarah arrives home, where Cathy and Victor inquire about her prolonged absence. Sarah explains to them,

"My car got damaged while I was returning home." Victor assures her, "Don't worry, Sarah, I'll handle it. Your car will be fixed by tomorrow morning."

It was a pleasant breezy morning. Sarah descends to the stairs, her mind consumed with thoughts of the tumultuous events in her life. She closes her eyes and savours the refreshing air, attempting to find solace for a brief moment. Afterwards, she sets off on the journey to Michael's house, lost in the thought about how much her life has changed. While driving, she gets lost in contemplation, contemplating the unpredictable twists and turns that have brought her to this point. Upon reaching Michael's place, she rings the doorbell, but there is no response. Frustrated, she pounds on the door, only to find it unlocked. She calls out,

"Dad, are you home?"

As she explores the hall, but there is no sign of anyone. She searches throughout the house before returning to the hall. However, something feels amiss, prompting her to retrace her steps and enter the bedroom. There, she discovers a few droplets of blood, assuming it may belong to Michael. Her expression turns grim as she desperately seeks further evidence, but her efforts prove fruitless. Feeling hopeless, she exits the house.

Sarah then contacts Jean, urgently requesting a meeting. Jean suggests meeting at her office to ensure the conversation remains confidential and free from prying eyes. Sarah agrees to Jean's suggestion. She arrives at the office and meets her, looking disturbed. Sensing Sarah's distress, Jean asks her to share her thoughts and explains

Dark Side of the New Year

why she appears so overwhelmed. Sarah provides a detailed account of the events, delving into the depths of her recent discoveries. Jean appears both surprised and anxious upon hearing that Michael is Sarah's biological father. She exclaims,

"What?! Give me a moment to process this information. How is this possible?"

Sarah confirms the truth of the matter and admits she is still trying to understand the situation herself. Jean, recognizing that Sarah is already burdened by her problems, decides not to disclose her investigation, which has uncovered some leads to the truth. Instead, Jean reassures Sarah, saying,

"Don't worry, dear. We will find Michael. I will take action in the investigation, but for now, you need to focus on your work as we also need to unravel Andrew's intentions."

Sarah acknowledges Jean's wisdom, agreeing, "Yes, Jean, you're right. I will take leave now. Goodbye! Please inform me if you discover anything about Michael."

Jean replies, "Of course, Sarah. Goodbye!"

Sarah arrives at the office, where Andrew questions her about her whereabouts. He expresses concern, stating that he called her multiple times. Sarah takes out her phone and realizes she missed several calls from Andrew. Apologetically, she explained that her phone was on silent. Andrew replies it's not a problem. He is worried about her well-being as she is still recovering. Sarah inquired if there was something urgent that required her immediate attention. Andrew responds affirmatively, sharing two important matters. Firstly, the investors have preponed the project deadline, which is now due by the end of the week, despite its Wednesday already. He suggests the possibility of extending shifts or working on the weekend. Sarah, maintaining a polite demeanour, reassures Andrew that she will manage within the designated shift timings, avoiding the need for extensions on weekdays or weekends. She then asks about the second matter. Andrew reveals that he heard rumours about her potential promotion. Sarah ponders, I have lost my father and these guys are worried about my promotion, like seriously? I can't trust anyone with this information not even Andrew Reminding herself to remain composed, she pretends to be excited about the promotion topic, masking her true emotions. Sarah feigns enthusiasm and says,

"Me? Am I the one who is going to be promoted?"

Andrew confirms the likelihood and suggests they focus on the project. Sarah agrees, and they continue their work. Meanwhile, Jean busily sifts through facts and organizes events chronologically to uncover the underlying truth. At the end of the day, Sarah receives a call from Nancy, who urgently requests her presence at her place. Concerned, Sarah asks Nancy about the situation, to which Nancy replies, urging her to come and mentioning that it involves their mother. Sarah assures Nancy not to worry and states she will be there soon.

Sarah arrives at Nancy's place to find the door open. As she enters the hall, she notices a doctor already present, examining Mehak aunt. Sarah calls out to Nancy, who rushes towards her for a hug. Sarah queries the situation, asking why the doctor is there. Nancy excitedly shares that her mother moved her hand today after enduring a long period of hardship. It's a moment of immense joy for Nancy, although her mother's attempts to speak are yet to be successful. Sarah, with a happy expression, celebrates the news and suggests they go meet her mother. They enter the room together and inquire about her health. The doctor informs them that Mehak is showing positive signs of recovery after approximately three months. Nancy expressed gratitude as she walked the doctor to the door.

Meanwhile, Sarah spoke to Mrs Bernard and offered words of hope and encouragement, assuring her that she would regain her ability to walk and carry on with life like before. Sarah turns toward the door, but Mehak holds her hand, trying to stop her. Overwhelmed with happiness, Sarah witnesses Mrs. Bernard's courage and determination to recover. She calls Nancy to share the moment and instructs her to take care of their mother. Sarah says bye to Nancy and drives to Jean's office.

Sarah enters Jean's office and enquires about Jean at the administration desk. The receptionist tells her that Jean is with a client at the moment and recommends that she wait. Sarah takes a seat and passes the time by reading a magazine that is available there. After thirty minutes, the meeting comes to an end, and then the receptionist leads Sarah to Jean's cabin. Excitedly, Sarah embraces Jean, holding both her hands tightly. She expresses her astonishment at Mehak aunt's responsive behaviour, sharing the news that she is now able to move her hand, and the doctor predicts a positive recovery if she continues with the same attitude. Jean responds with enthusiasm,

"Oh, Sarah! That's truly wonderful news amidst all the despair. I hope aunt recovers soon."

Sarah takes a deep breath, and suddenly, a wave of darkness washes over her face as thoughts of Michael consume her. Tears well up in her eyes, and she exclaims,

"DAD!"

The tears stream down her face uncontrollably. Jean comforted Sarah and promised to uncover the mystery. Sarah embraces Jean and utters, "Jean, I've lost all hope and courage to find the truth." Jean spoke in a calming tone and encouraged the her to avoid negativity. Jean uses evidence and finds more clues to help Sarah feel better about finding the truth. Recognizing that it has been a long day for Sarah, Jean suggests she take some rest. Sarah agrees, says bye, and heads home. Despite feeling angry with her parents for hiding the truth about Michael, Sarah puts on a fake smile. Cathy helps her take her medication, and then the whole family comes together to chat. As midnight approaches, Sarah falls asleep on the couch. Lovingly, Cathy gently kisses Sarah's forehead before going to bed.

Sarah had a tiring day and overslept the next morning, which delayed her by about two hours. She hurried to get ready, as she was late for work and had to finish a project by the end of the week. Despite her efforts, she couldn't make it on time and arrived an hour late at the office. When Sarah arrived late, her project team members were surprised and disappointed. They pointed to their watches as a reminder of her tardiness. Sarah apologized for the delay and told them that she was having a difficult time. She promises to extend her working hours by an additional hour to make up for the delay. Each team member responded individually, providing words of empathy and encouragement. They assured her that everyone experiences difficulties in life.

They pledge to work together to complete the project. With her teammates convinced, Sarah felt a sigh of relief.

Meanwhile, Andrew enters the meeting room where Sarah and the team are working. They were simultaneously inquired about their delayed joining. They chuckled while changing glances in response. Sarah told Andrew that it had been a tiring day for her and she felt dizzy, which caused her to be late. Andrew smiled and shared that he had arrived early to utilize the time to speak to their boss about the project. Sarah playfully admits her mistake, and Andrew pats her back, assuring her not to worry. They rally the team together to focus on their work.

The team members immerse themselves deeply in the project, displaying a great passion for their work. They conduct extensive research on designs, trends, communication, and personal development. Importantly, their contentment aligns with their work. At the end of the day, their hard work pays off, generating innovative ideas for the project. Their faces radiate genuine happiness as they celebrate briefly before leaving the office one by one.

But Sarah is still sad inside, dealing with thoughts of her father who is missing. She exits the office and settles into her car. She cries out loud, wondering why her father disappeared, especially now that she knows the truth after so many years. She hopes Jean might have some answers, so she decides to call. She sees 10 missed calls from the

Dark Side of the New Year

previous night, which shocks her, causing her to drop the phone. For a moment, she feels confused and finds it hard to breathe. She can't make sense of her emotions because all the missed calls were from "Michael."

She musters up the courage to call back and, in a terrified voice, utters,

"Hello, Dad, is this you?"

A male voice from the other end confirms, "Yes, my dear, it's me. Where have you been? Why didn't you make it yesterday? I was trying to contact you..."

Sarah explains, "Dad, I did visit your place, but the door was open, and no one was home. I also noticed a few drops of blood, which worried me. I informed Jean, my childhood best friend, who is a lawyer."

Michael becomes concerned about Sarah's well-being and responds, "My love, you didn't come here. I was home all the time waiting for you!"

Both of them are stressed by the events of the previous day, he inquire about the recent dream she had, which gives Sarah a hint about the incident. In a frightened voice, she exclaims,

"Damn! am I just imagining things? Dad, please help me!"

Dark Side of the New Year

Michael advises her to return home for the day, take her medicine, and rest without dwelling on any other thoughts. He reassures her, saying, "Don't worry, dear. We will meet tomorrow morning. I'll be downstairs at your place to pick you up at 8 a.m. Text me your address." Sarah bids him good night and sends her address. She then calls Jean to update her on the incident, and Jean advises her to rest.

The following day, Sarah wakes up with the sunrise, eagerly anticipating the meeting with her father to reminisce about their golden days and discuss the events of the past years. She starts her usual routine, including a gym session, she gets dressed and prepares breakfast for the family. They all have breakfast together and start their day. Sarah leaves the house early, driven by her eagerness to see her dad. She waits downstairs as instructed by Michael, who arrives an hour earlier than scheduled. Sarah sits in the car and hugs her dad, and they engage in a conversation about her hallucinations, which continues until they reach Michael's place. They arrive within 15 minutes due to the absence of traffic on the early morning road. Michael prepares coffee for both of them and praises it by saying,

"Your mom used to love the coffee I made. It was my duty."

Sarah smiles and asks him to tell her more about her mom. Michael gladly obliges, and they both take a seat on the couch. While sipping her favourite coffee, Michael starts talking about his wife, displaying her picture. He describes her as Amanda, the most beautiful lady he had ever seen before Sarah's birth. He recounts how they met at a New Year party through a mutual friend, where he was immediately captivated by her. He is in awe that Sarah looks like a replica of Amanda. They initiated a conversation during a game of truth and dare, in which Sarah's mom asked him,

"Who is the prettiest lady you have ever seen?"

Michael smirked and replied, "Ever since I saw her, I haven't been able to blink my eyes. I'm still looking into her eyes."

This marked the beginning of their friendship, and they started spending time together, watching movies, going hiking, and satisfying their shared passion for travel. Over time, their friendship blossomed into love, and they got married within a year. Michael reveals that he had betrayed her years later because of another girl whom he loved more than her. Sarah interjects, exclaiming,

"What?"

Michael laughs and responds, "That was you, my love!" Both of them share a smile.

Michael proceeds with his story, saying, "A few months later, after all those joyful moments, a dark night descended upon our family. It was a night when dusky clouds cast their shadow, and your mom suddenly puked blood. I was shattered into pieces witnessing that sight. I rushed her to the hospital immediately, where the doctors speculated it might be hematemesis but required further tests to confirm the illness." Michael's voice trembles and tears stream down his face as he continues, "The doctors conducted all the necessary tests, and the results made the ground slip from under my feet." Sarah attempts to calm him down, gently patting his back and fetching a glass of water. She reassures him, "Dad, if you need a break, please go get some fresh air. I have been unaware of so many things all these years, and I don't want you to suffer more." Michael is unable to utter a single word and silently nods his head before leaving the room.

As he departs, Sarah falls to the ground and breaks into tears. After a while, she reminds herself that it is not the time to succumb to her emotions; she needs to support her dad. With this thought in mind, she runs towards the door, searching for him. Unable to find him, she explores the neighbourhood and discovers a backyard attached to the house. Stepping into the backyard, she is shocked to find him sitting near a cemetery. Sarah speaks in a low and scared voice,

Dark Side of the New Year

"Dad, what are you doing here?"

Michael turns around, tears streaming down his face, and responds, "Dear, here is your mom. I never wanted to part ways with her, so I buried her here in the backyard, allowing me to talk to her whenever I want."

Sarah's face reflects a mixture of shock and disturbance as she asks him, "Dad, please come inside the house." Both of them re-enter the home.

Sarah urges Michael to sit on the couch and brings him a glass of water. Speaking calmly, she asks,

"Dad, are you okay? What is all this? How could you keep Mom's remains in the backyard? That's not the appropriate way to honour her memory!"

Michael replies in a sobbing voice, "I don't know how this happened to your mom. She was a happy person, and..." He breaks down in tears, and Sarah tries to comfort him by patting his back. She prepares a cup of coffee for him. It takes several minutes for Sarah to console him, but eventually, he composes himself enough to answer her questions. Michael says, "Dear, you deserve to know everything about your mom. The test results revealed that she had advanced-stage blood cancer. It devastated both of us to see such a fate befall a vibrant and compassionate person. Your mom had a heart of gold. She provided free food packets to the homeless every night on the streets, organized charity events where people donated their reusable clothes to the underprivileged, and I supported her wholeheartedly in all these endeavours. After receiving the diagnosis, we made a conscious decision to cherish the time we had left together, to savour the moments rather than dwelling on sadness and succumbing to despair. We created a bucket list of places to visit since both your mother and I had a deep love for travel and exploration. At the top of our list were destinations such as India, Venice, experiencing the cherry blossom in Japan, Bora Bora, and Niagara Falls in the USA."

"We travelled to all these places, and during Japan's cherry blossom season, your mother appeared like an angel to me, which brought tears to my eyes at the thought of losing her. However, I witnessed the happiest expression on her face, which compelled me to hold myself together so that she wouldn't feel any sadness because of me. On that day, your mom wrote a poem for me that once again stirred my emotions, and this time, I couldn't hold myself." Curious, Sarah asks, "What was the poem, Dad?" Michael begins reciting the poem; his voice filled with emotions.

Dark Side of the New Year

Upon the day I first beheld your grace,

My heart did skip a beat and quickened its pace.

Each time you neared, breathless it became,

A momentary pause in passion's flame.

I sought to rein my emotions, keep them at bay,

But futile were my efforts; they refused to sway.

For deep within my soul, love did reside,

Unable to conceal, it could not hide.

In secret rendezvous, away from prying eyes,

I cherished every second as time swiftly flew.

Longing to clasp your hand for all eternity,

In that fleeting moment, love found its serenity.

Yet now, alas, our paths are bound to sever,

Dark Side of the New Year

With each passing day, my heart breaks, aching forever.

But amidst the darkness, a glimmer still gleams,

Hope resides within Sofia, the realm of dreams.

You were not my first love, but you shall be my last,

Though you tried to instil hatred in me, so vast.

I comprehend your worries, your fears,

Yet, despite your foolishness, I shan't shed any tears.

Now that I have entrusted my heart to you,

I shall embrace this love, forever true.

With unwavering trust, I shall hold it tight,

For you, my love, through each day and night.

Tears cascaded down Sarah's cheeks as she uttered, "This poem has touched my heart! But dad, who is Sofia?" Michael tenderly replied, "That was your childhood name, dear. Your guardians may have changed it to Sarah."

Riddhi Joshi

Dark Side of the New Year

Overwhelmed with emotion, Sarah sobbed and expressed, "Dad, I had a dream a few days ago where someone called me by the name Sofia." Michael hugged her tightly, offering solace, and handed her a glass of water.

Gathering her composure, Sarah tells Michael,

"Dad, please tell me more. I want to know everything."

Michael began recounting their story, "After hearing your mom's poem, we clung to one another, tears of sorrow streaming down our faces. We remained locked in that hug until we were urged to leave. Upon concluding our travels, we returned home and rested for two days. Then, your mom insisted I return to the office. Reluctantly, I left home. It was during this time that your mom received a call from her best friend, inviting her for a shopping trip. Being a skilled driver, she left alone. Unfortunately, she experienced dizziness while on the highway, resulting in a devastating collision with a truck. She was taken from me in an instant. The accident was horrendous, and your mom's face was barely recognizable. Only her identification documents and phone allowed the authorities to identify her. Since then, I have blamed myself for leaving home. A month later, a woman named Lucie entered my life. We met at a wedding, and she expressed her feelings for me. I informed her about Amanda, and although she was intrigued, she vowed to wait until I had moved on. She began following me on social media and connected with me. Though she possessed a beautiful heart, I loved Amanda and had no desire for another partner. But one night, I had a dream. I found myself beneath the cherry blossom trees with Amanda beside me. She said, 'Always remember your promise!' I awoke from my slumber, unable to sleep for the remaining of the night."

Dark Side of the New Year

Chapter 7
An Attempt To Murder

Curiosity burning within her, Sarah inquired,

"What promise did you make to Mom?"

Michael replied, reminiscing, "During our visit to witness Japan's cherry blossom, I shared the poem with you. On that evening, as the weather turned from a romantic and delightful cherry blossom scene to a cloudy and windy atmosphere, your mom spoke to me. She acknowledged my deep love for her and knew that I would never fall in love with anyone else. However, she believed that you needed a mother's love and care. I suggested hiring a babysitter, but she rejected all my ideas and extracted a promise from me. I vowed to marry someone who could love and care for you, Sarah."

Sarah's phone began incessantly ringing. Concerned, Michael inquired about the continuous interruptions. Sarah explained,

"We have a project deadline today that requires submission to the investors. I need to leave for the office now. My colleagues must be waiting for me to finalize the project; and my promotion will be based on the project"

Understanding the situation, Michael advised, "Dear, it seems you need to leave for your office. Your colleagues are likely awaiting your presence to complete the project. We can reconvene this evening."

Sarah replied, "sure, dad! I'll make every effort to arrive as soon as possible." With those words, Sarah leaves from her father and departed for the office, hailing a cab for her journey.

Upon Sarah's arrival at the office, Andrew inquires, "Sarah, where have you been? You're half an hour late." Her face looked quite dull and she replies, can we focus on the work now rather than discussing about me being late for a while. Andrew senses that Sarah is going through with some undisclosed issues and decides not to press further. He agrees, saying, "Of course, love! Let's finalize everything." The team unites, pooling their efforts to set their plans into action. All the designs were finalised and went for stitching the last day, which were made overnight, they are now prepared to showcase their creations to the investors. A grand fashion show has been arranged for the models to exhibit the designs at noon.

Sarah and Andrew begin the task of assigning dresses to the models, carefully determining which outfits suits each individual. This process took nearly two hours before they reach a conclusion. The time for the show has arrived. The models grace the stage one after another, flaunting meticulously crafted designs. The show turns out to be an extraordinary success, impressing the investors with the designs and their impeccable presentation. Although they had already invested in the project, the investors offered a staggering $50 million to the company. Sarah's work and her exceptional sense of fashion and design have left everyone in awe. The team and investors express their appreciation for her outstanding work. To commemorate the triumph, they decide to celebrate over lunch at a fine dining restaurant, raising a toast to Sarah. Her boss addresses the gathering, saying,

Dark Side of the New Year

"Ladies and gentlemen, may I have your attention, please! I am delighted to announce that this project has been a resounding success, thanks to your hard work and dedication. I assure you all that those involved in this venture will receive an additional bonus this year!"

The room erupts in cheers of joy.

The boss continues, "Furthermore, I have another announcement. Our esteemed project host, Sarah, has shown exceptional resilience despite personal hardships. In light of her extraordinary dedication and contributions to this project, I am pleased to announce her promotion. Starting next month, she will be on the position of a buyer, responsible for finalizing all the designs. Congratulations, Sarah! You have truly earned it!"

The room fills with congratulations, and they proceed to enjoy their meal. Subsequently, one by one, they depart from the restaurant.

Andrew turns to Sarah and says,

"Sarah, can I drop you home? It has been quite a while since we spent time together."

Sarah's mind is consumed with thoughts of meeting her father and learning every detail about him. However, refusing Andrew's offer could jeopardize her and Jean's plan of feigning a romantic relationship. She contemplates and then replies,

"Sure, Andrew. I was thinking the same."

They leave from the restaurant together in his car, where soft melodious tunes fill the air. To add to the ambience, rainfall commences, enhancing the romantic atmosphere. Andrew serenades her with a song, prompting Sarah to compliment him, saying,

"You could have pursued a second career in singing, Andrew!"

They both smiles before arriving at Sarah's home. Andrew drops her off downstairs, hugs her, and leaves, saying, "Goodbye, Sarah. Have a good day, and once again, congratulations on your promotion!"

Sarah reciprocates, "Thank you, Andrew. Have a great day ahead!" Sarah drives her car and heads towards Michael's place. She sends a text message to her mother, informing her that she will be late or possibly arrive in the morning due to important matters requiring her attention. Her mother responds,

"Sure, dear. Take care!"

Dark Side of the New Year

Sarah arrives at Michael's place and exclaims,

"Dad, I'm home!"

As he opens the door, he collapses onto Sarah, causing her to try to support him. She notices a knife protruding from his back, causing a continuous flow of blood. Sarah in a frightened voice asks,

"What happened, Dad? Who did this to you? I'm taking you to the hospital; I can't bear the thought of losing you so suddenly!"

At that moment, it feels like a vital part of her life is slipping away. Sarah assists Michael to her car, settling him in the front seat and removing the knife before securing his seatbelt. She drives with reckless abandon, her sole focus fixed on reaching the hospital in time to save her father. She completes the 20-minute journey in just 10 minutes, rushing toward the hospital and desperately screaming for help. The hospital staff gazes at her in alarm, but suddenly the doctor who had previously treated Sarah arrives and instructs the staff to attend to the emergency case. Without hesitation, the staff swiftly transports Michael to the emergency ward. Meanwhile, Sarah fervently prays for her father's recovery, her eyes filled with tears.

An hour later, the doctor emerges from the operating theatre, prompting Sarah to inquire anxiously,

"Doctor, how is he? Is he alright?"

The doctor replies, "Yes, he is now out of danger, and, fortunately, he has regained consciousness."

Sarah expresses her gratitude, saying, "Thank you, doctor, for saving his life. Will he be discharged today?"

The doctor reassures her, saying, "Yes, Sarah, you may take your friend home. Just ensure he takes the prescribed medication as instructed."

Sarah responds, "Certainly, doctor. Thank you so much!"

She supports Michael as he leans on her shoulder, helping him walk to the car and securing his seatbelt. They journey back home in tranquillity. Sarah administers the prescribed medication and assists Michael in settling down for sleep. The following morning, she fills the entire house with the aroma of green tea and cake. They begin the day with a simple breakfast, followed by Michael's medication. He suggests Sarah return home, mentioning that Cathy and Victor might be concerned. However, Sarah refuses, stating,

"Dad, in this situation, I cannot leave you alone. I'll text Mom to let her know I won't be coming home today." She proceeds to send a message to Cathy. Simultaneously,

Dark Side of the New Year

Marc calls Victor and says, "Hello, are you Sarah's father?" Victor confirms his identity and inquiries about the reason for the call. In an expression of concern, Marc says, "We need to double Sarah's dosage as she came to the hospital yesterday, pleading for her friend's life." Unfortunately, the tragic part is that she was alone. Her hallucinations have escalated to an alarming level. We need to take care of her." Victor responds with a worried tone, "Okay, doctor. I will follow your instructions. Thank you."

As Sarah's curiosity about her birth parents intensifies, she asks her father,

"Are you feeling better, Dad?"

Michael senses his daughter's eagerness to learn the rest of the story and responds,

"Yes, dear, I'm feeling much better now. Let me continue the story. As I dreamt of Amanda, memories flooded my mind—moments of joy and happiness that adorned our faces. We cherished every occasion with radiant smiles. Oh, it was a nostalgic moment for me! Suddenly, it struck me that the dream had a purpose, which led me to Lucie! As I promised your mother, I was meant to marry someone who could provide you with a motherly love. So, I decided to be with Lucie, and we began dating. We devoted time to understanding each other's preferences, tastes, and perspectives on life. My first question to her was,

'Will you be able to take care of my daughter?'

Her answer left me amazed and filled with care. She said,

'I will take care of our daughter, not just yours!'

At that very moment, I knew I wanted to marry her, although I didn't share my true intentions at that moment. I simply smiled and responded, 'That's wonderful! How considerate of you.' She replied, 'Michael, I love you with all my heart, ever since I laid eyes on you!' We had dinner together that evening, and I escorted her home. A few days later, she proposed and I gladly married her."

I was fully engrossed in my work, relying on her to take care of you in the background. She made a significant aspect of my life easier, allowing me to dedicate my time to business development. I ventured into the perfume production industry, founding a company that experienced tremendous success. Subsequently, I launched several other brands. The company where you currently work was established by me, my dear. Back then, I became a role model for many. The key reason behind my business success was Lucie, as she assisted in your growth, guiding you from holding your fingers in the crib to crawling on your own.

Dark Side of the New Year

On a business trip, I was at ease, believing Lucie was there to care for you. However, one day, I returned home to surprise Lucie, only to witness a distressing and unbelievable scene. Lucie was present in my house with lawyers and cops. When I inquired about the situation, my mind was overwhelmed by the shocking revelation. I felt utterly helpless and unable to process anything. Naturally, I was also worried about you.

The reason for their presence at my residence was that Lucie had filed for divorce, alleging that I had attempted to murder her father. I pleaded with the cops, questioning why I would harm my father-in-law, but my words fell on deaf ears. They claimed to possess a confession from her father and considered Lucie, a witness. I was unjustly imprisoned for ten long years for a crime I never committed, as all the evidence seemed to be against me. Lucie demanded 75% of my property and business as a condition to care for you in my absence. Desperate to provide you with the best, I signed all the papers, surrendering everything I had. However, Lucie played a double game. She requested the court to award custody of you to any relatives or place you in an orphanage. That's when I managed to persuade Cathy and Victor to adopt you. They, too, were swayed by Lucie's fabricated case and couldn't trust my innocence.

Every day spent in prison, I counted the moments until I could see you, love you, and witness your growth. Each day felt like a year as I eagerly awaited your presence. I prayed for your well-being daily, clinging to the hope of seeing you upon my release. The sole purpose that kept me alive throughout those years was the anticipation of your smile and embrace. However, a decade later, when the time came for our reunion, I hurried to Victor's place, only to find the door locked. I enquired with the neighbours, but nobody had any information. No one knew anything. Desperate for leads, I questioned everyone on every floor of the building. Eventually, I learned from someone that a tragic accident had claimed the lives of all three of them. Hearing this news, I collapsed to my knees. My world crumbled, and I felt utterly helpless. I screamed out your name repeatedly, but the long-awaited day I had yearned for had become meaningless, replaced only by sorrow in my life. I was shattered, unsure of what to do next. I wandered the streets aimlessly, spending the entire day in despair. I slept on the pavement, resembling a beggar. I had neither a roof over my head nor bread to sustain me.

A few days later, a gentleman approached me while I was seated on the street. He inquired if I was Michael, the renowned business tycoon. With tears in my eyes, I replied, "No, I am Michael, but I am no longer the business tycoon. I have neither a place to stay nor food to eat." He revealed himself as a devoted fan and expressed his willingness to help. Being a manager at a taxi company, he managed to secure a job for me as a taxi driver. He kindly allowed me to

Dark Side of the New Year

stay at his place until I received my first salary. Subsequently, I rented my current residence, and I have been staying here since then. I am grateful to the man who supported me during the darkest period of my life.

Sarah, embracing her father, expresses her anger-filled eyes, exclaiming, "I will avenge Lucie for destroying your life, Dad." He responds with a smile, saying, "My dear, it's a complicated story from the past. Destiny plays a significant role. Please don't worry about it." Concerned, Sarah asks her father, "Dad, who tried to stab you with a knife the other day?" After contemplating for a moment with a frowned face he replies, "I don't know, dear. The attacker came from behind, and I couldn't see the face." Sarah asks Michael to rest upstairs and appears worried about finding the culprit and decides to call Jean to her father's place, urgently requesting her presence. She informs Jean of the urgency and texts her the address. Jean responds with optimism.

Chapter 8
Paying For Your Sins

As Jean leaves her home, the weather takes an unexpected turn. The calm and pleasant atmosphere, with gentle cold breezes brushing through her hair, has changed to heavy rainfall. The sky looks dark and sad, as if crying with tears, forming cloud patterns resembling a human face. Jean adjusts the car's speed, driving cautiously within the speed limit. It takes nearly an hour for her to reach Michael's place. Sarah, anxiously rushes towards Jean upon her arrival, and asks if she encountered any problems on the way. Jean places her hands on Sarah's shoulders, reassuring her with a

Dark Side of the New Year

smile, "Don't worry, dear, I'm fine. How about you? You seem quite disturbed." She encourages Sarah to take a seat.

Sarah proceeds to explain every detail, recounting how she found her father stabbed and sharing the love story. When Jean hears the name Lucie, her reaction is disturbed, and she exclaims sharply, "Lucie?" Sarah appears perplexed by Jean's response and asks,

"What happened, Jean? Do you know her?"

Jean gazes at her for a moment and says, "Sarah, I need to share something crucial with you. I have been trying to uncover the truth from various angles and have stumbled upon some unbelievable facts. A few days ago, I visited Nancy's place to see her mom and spend time with her. During that visit, Mr. Bernard unexpectedly joined us and asked me for a coffee. Accidentally, I dropped his wallet, and when I picked it up, I noticed a picture inside with the name 'Lucie' mentioned. It's the same woman whose picture you sent me, the one Andrew met!" Sarah appears greatly surprised.

Jean adds, "In addition, I sent someone to follow Mr. Bernard and they sent me a photo of the same woman at a location outside the city where he met her. I strongly suspect there is a relationship between them, and we need to investigate further." Sarah expresses her confusion and says, "I'm not sure what's going on, but there seems to be something ominous happening that we're not aware of." Jean's voice grows louder as she speaks, emphasizing, "Exactly! Misfortune seems to have surrounded Aunt Mehak as well. When I met her, she gripped my hand tightly with her last finger. I sensed she was trying to convey something, so I asked her if she had something to say. She responded with a 'yes.' I asked if it pertained to her, and again, she replied 'yes.' I was perplexed, wondering what she was trying to express. A couple of minutes later, she gestured towards a picture with her eyes. I turned to look and was surprised to see that she was pointing at her husband. I asked her if she wanted me to call Mr. Bernard, but her tear-filled eyes pleaded 'no.' That made me suspicious, and I started asking her more questions in an attempt to uncover the truth. I asked if it had something to do with both of them, and she replied, 'Yes.' I questioned whether he had done something wrong to her, and she affirmed it. I grew concerned for Aunt, but suddenly, Mr. Bernard entered the room, and I couldn't inquire further. He invited me for coffee, and the wallet incident occurred."

Sarah asks Jean if she has any idea about what might have happened. Jean responds, "No, but the fear in Mehak Aunt's eyes was undeniable. Something is amiss in that place. From my observations and beliefs, there is a connection between

Dark Side of the New Year

Lucie and Mr. Bernard. We need to keep an eye on Mr. Bernard and his intentions."

The team devised a strategy. Michael would observe Andrew, Sarah would keep an eye on Lucie, and Jean would investigate Mr. Bernard. Jean asked Sarah to inform the plan to Michael. She agreed before they each went to keep an eye on their respective targets. Meanwhile, Michael rests at home for a while, planning to leave after an hour of rest.

Jean arrives at the Bernard's residence, but Mr. Bernard is not present. She sits with Mrs. Bernard and attempts to communicate with her. Jean narrates the entire story to Aunt Mehak and informs her that she will be back from the restroom. In the meantime, Mr. Bernard returns home and notices Mehak struggling to move her hand and utter words. With a wicked smile, he approaches the side table and says,

"Mehak, you can speak now! How amazing! But no more!"

He picks up a flower vase from the side table, intending to strike her. To his surprise, Mrs. Bernard holds the vase with her hand and rises from the bed. She says in a loud voice,

"Not anymore, Vance! You will have to face the consequences of your sins! It ends now."

At that moment, Jean enters the room, sending shivers down Mr. Bernard's spine. He questions,

"Jean, what are you doing here?"

She calmly responds, "I came to visit Aunt Mehak, but it seems she is doing well now. It's a heartwarming sight."

Vance, wearing a wide smile, expresses his satisfaction, saying, "Yes, I'm delighted to see Mehak's recovery."

Jean's voice rises with anger as she exclaims, "Stop lying, Mr. Bernard. I know the truth about how Aunt Mehak became paralyzed, everything about Lucie, and all your sins."

Mr. Bernard's face transitions from relief to a composed demeanour, and he retorts, "Ah, that's great. I won't have to pretend anymore. But there's nothing you can do about it. You have no evidence of me pushing Mehak from the terrace."

Suddenly, Sarah and Michael arrive at the location accompanied by the cops, who have handcuffed Lucie and Andrew. Confused, Vance asks, "What's happening here? Why are the cops here?" One of the officers' replies, "Vance, you're under arrest for your crimes," and proceeds to place handcuffs on him.

Dark Side of the New Year

Jean speaks with a confident and assertive tone, addressing Mr. Bernard, "I understand it must be difficult for you to understand how your scheme was exposed. Let me enlighten you. Do you recall when I visited your house, and you offered me coffee? On that day, while conversing with Aunt Mehak, she started responding to my words. Despite her stuttering, she managed to answer my questions. That's when I discovered your true nature. She revealed me about how she got paralysed that day as she came to know about you and Lucie, being a stoned person, you pushed her from the terrace to keep her shut forever. Fortunately, she survived. We devised a plan for Aunt Mehak to pretend to be paralyzed to expose you. Subsequently, Sarah contacted me to meet her, and I shared the details of my conversation with Aunt Mehak. Later, I informed the cops about the entire case. Given my profession as a lawyer, they trusted my account even without substantial evidence and assisted in gathering it."

"We all gathered at Lucie's residence, and her astonishment was palpable when she saw us accompanied by the cops. Upon entering her home, we inquired about the entire case. Initially, she remained silent until I disclosed that we were fully aware of the attempted murder of Aunt Mehak by you and Mr. Bernard. We informed her that we possessed strong evidence, and Aunt Mehak has recovered and provided us with full details. Thus, there was no benefit in concealing anything. However, if she chose to divulge the truth, we could potentially offer some leniency during her imprisonment."

Lucie began revealing the truth in an attempt to absolve herself from the situation. She begins her story by stating that Vance had always loved Amanda, while she reciprocated feelings for Michael, which greatly affected him. Consequently, Vance decided to make Amanda's life a living hell. However, fate had different plans in store for her, as she became afflicted with cancer, yet Vance's humanity failed to manifest.

Do you truly believe it was a mere accident?

That notion is quite foolish. It was Vance who was behind the wheel of that truck, deliberately taking her life as an act of revenge, even though he never expressed his feelings to Amanda. Following that incident, he spiralled into a state of psychological instability. He subsequently made a plan to make Michael's life unbearable, hiring me to feign love for Michael and compensating me generously for my role. I did everything for the sake of Michael, and then I accused him of attempting to murder my father according to Bernard's plot. We seized all of Michael's assets and business, in which Vance held a 70% stake. We manipulated Cathy and Victor into believing that Michael had committed the crime. Eventually, we convinced them to take Sofia with them following the court hearing. We secured a new residence for them and fabricated a fictional narrative about the family's demise, even changing Sofia's name to Sarah to ensure Michael would never discover his daughter's whereabouts."

"Vance later married Mehak, and a year later, I cannot recall when exactly Vance and I fell in love with each other and conceived Andrew. Once we learned about Andrew's friendship with Sarah, we divulged the entire story to him and asked him to distance himself from her. However, Andrew's mind was fixated on killing Sarah, as she reminded him of Amanda. He devised a plan to feign love for her. The accident that caused her hallucinations was intentionally orchestrated by Andrew. When Mehak discovered our relationship, Vance attempted to end her life by pushing her from the terrace. Unfortunately, she survived, albeit paralyzed."

It is important to note that Lucie's statement has been recorded, as well as your own. You confessed to the crime few moments ago.

Mr. Bernard, facing the presence of the cops, attempts to hit Lucie as she confessed everything. The officers hold him back for a moment and then head towards the exit to take all three of them to jail. But Vance keeps trying to reach his pocket, and eventually, he pulls out a knife attempting to harm Sarah. The officer quickly grabs his hand, giving him a hard slap before arresting him. Amid the chaos, Sarah realizes Michael is missing and asks Jean,

"Have you seen Michael?"

Jean replies, "No, dear, you arrived here alone."

Hearing this, Sarah becomes anxious and swiftly moves out of the place. She heads towards Michael's residence, searching every corner, but finds the house deserted. She sits on the couch, contemplating where he could be. Suddenly, a gust of wind causes the curtains to flutter, drawing attention to her mother's cemetery. She makes her way there and takes a seat, reflecting in silence. Amidst the quietude, she hears a cat's meow emanating from behind the cemetery. Curiosity piques her interest, leading her towards the feline. She cradles the cat in her arms and holds it close.

Looking at the cemetery, she accidentally drops the cat, causing her to stumble and fall to her knees. As she reads the inscription on the tombstone, it says:

"In the loving memory of Amanda and Michael."

Overwhelmed by emotion, Sarah flees from the site and rushes to her car. She can only hear a voice saying,

"My love, the day I learned of your demise, I chose to end my own life."

Dark Side of the New Year

She cries out in pain and drives to the Seine River, where she stays for hours, unable to stop her tears. Eventually, she drifts into sleep on a bench.

The morning sun's rays gently touch her face, and she wakes up to hear Michael's voice cheering her on, "Be happy, my love. You still have your life, and we want you to be strong. Make us proud instead of dwelling on the painful truth." Gazing up at the sky with teary eyes, she replies, "Yes, Dad, I will." Just like the morning sun brings new hope, Sarah begins a journey to rebuild her life. As time passes, she finds comfort and starts seeing things in a new way.

Dark Side of the New Year

www.ingramcontent.com/pod-product-compliance
Lightning Source LLC
LaVergne TN
LVHW030344070526
838199LV00067B/6439